Praise for the Series

"The characters are bold and vibrant, the dragon adores pie, and the magic is every bit as wondrous as you'd find in any epic fantasy tale." —L.L. MacRae, author of *The Dragon Spirits*

"Cheeky, sharp, humorous, Pratchett-esque. A bit silly, but in the best way possible." —Andy Peloquin, bestselling author of the *Darkblade* series

"Delightful and fun." —K.E. Andrews, SPFBO 9 finalist and author of *Hills of Heather and Bone*

"The size of the novel is short but the humor is big." —Laura Huie, author of *The Sunset Sovereign: A Dragon's Memoir*

"A thoroughly enjoyable little tale of a little girl, a little dragon and their quest for a big future together!" —Sue Bavey, author of *Kookaburras, Cuppas & Kangaroos*

"A fun, cozy fantasy with just the right amount of tension." —Cat Bowser, author of *Mirrors and Ashes*

"It's heartwarming, it's funny, it's thrilling, it's refreshing, and, most of all, it's absolutely unforgettable!" —Esmay Rosalyne, Before We Go Blog

"I loved just about everything about this book. It felt like chicken soup for my soul." —The Literary Apothecary

Dragon Along
The Dragons of Nóra, Book Two
Joseph John Lee

Eclipseborn Publishing

Book Cover by Miblart

First edition 2025

For Cam and Alice

May all your adventures make for the best stories

Prologue

On the whole, the Priory of the Thrice-Dead Prophet was unbothered by the existence of dragons and found the Inquisitors that borrowed its namesake to be rather a nuisance. What truly ruffled its feathers were the fae, but one could make the argument that presiding over one Inquisition was more than enough while starting a second was just being greedy.

While dragons had long been tied to Nóra and her people, the fae inhabitants of the land were a more mysterious sort. They lacked the cultural significance held by dragons, and instead, they were held in quieter regard, believed to be tricksters, thieves, malcontents, and generally unpleasant to be around.

Though that would depend on who you'd ask, and if you were only asking about gnomes. Those guys were jerks.

The fact of the matter is, those who would be in the know of the activities of fae were those who found themselves living far from those who were curious enough to ask about them. Meanwhile, the loudest voices were often those belonging to the Priory.

Why the Priory was so steadfast against the existence of the fae was anyone's guess. Priory officials claimed it was to ensure the safety of the land of Nóra. Inquisitors would accuse the Priory of stealing their motivation. The Priory would accuse the Inquisition of attaching themselves to their name for no good reason. The questions would often go nowhere.

All anyone could say for certain was that the fae were often found in woodland areas far from human settlements, the Priory instituted a ban on fae research and storytelling, and no one particularly cared to enforce that ban outside of the capital city of Mór.

One could consider such a development fortunate, because so long as no one brings this tale to Mór, the Priory will not stomp their feet about it.

Chapter One

Dragons, meanwhile, were still technically banned throughout Nóra, though given none had been seen in generations until about a week or two ago, it was easier to keep one's eyes shut and pretend it was working.

When two dragons hatch over the course of a week, however, it tended to throw a wrench in those plans.

Camaráin didn't care for those plans, though. The wee boy, only eight years of age but having just returned from the adventure of a lifetime, certainly would not have imagined being anything of a disruption beyond the usual grief-giving to his ma. But here he sat in his bedroom, empty but for the bed in front of him and the stacks of books in the corner left to him by his uncle, and silent but for the wind whistling outside throughout the village of Baile and the rather distracting cracking of the dragon egg hatching on his bed. One could not exactly divert their attention from something like that.

After all, it's not every day you watch a dragon egg crack open until it covers your bedsheets in a smattering of shards and a viscous goo, even if did seem that way recently. It was easy for Camaráin to ignore that as he eyed the dragon that emerged from it.

Small, beady eyes opened as the hatchling let loose a low grumble, much deeper than the trills and squawks Camaráin's sister's dragon often made. Its scales were a deep red, glinting like rubies. As it looked up at the boy, it tried to rise to its legs, only to fall back into the puddle of its own making with a wet splat.

Camaráin stifled a chuckle, intent on not alerting his ma to anything amiss. Part of him was eager to show her the egg—back when he had no inkling as to when it would actually hatch—but to show her *another* dragon, so soon after leaving Ailís in the Draconic Highlands with Uncle Iósaf and a host of ancient dragons to train her in the way of Bonded magic? There was a time and place for everything, and this was neither. He knew she'd need some time.

For now, though, he was all too excited to pick the hatchling off his bed, a smile wide. He reached toward the dragon—male, it was clear—and wrapped eager hands around his small frame. The scales were warm to the touch, far more than those of Pilib, his sister's dragon. The hatchling's eyes lit with a friendly warmth that Camaráin was all too intent to match, enough for him to ignore how gross and damp the newborn felt. He held him at eye level, baring his teeth with glee, and he danced in place in a rough approximation of the dance lessons Ailís never went to.

Chuckling, he opened his mouth to say his first words to the dragon, to welcome him to this world.

He just didn't expect his bedroom door to fly open before he got the chance.

"Camaráin, do you know why all the pie tins are—" Ma froze in the doorway, her hair tied back in a messy bun, loose strands indicating she had been lying in bed. Her mouth fell agape, one hand raised and holding a pie tin that appeared to have had a chunk bitten off. She pointed at Camaráin and the dragon with her free hand, and whatever emotions were in her eyes, they were too numerous for Cam to discern.

Glancing between the hatchling and his ma, he forced a smile and said, "This isn't the worst thing I've brought home."

Ma raised her eyebrow and dropped her arms, the pie tin clanging against the doorframe. "Really?" she deadpanned. "And what *is* the worst thing, then?"

"Remember when I brought that beehive inside with me?"

Grumbling, Ma said, "Do I ever." A pair of bees buzzed past her as if on cue, and she flinched and screamed on instinct. "It's been three years and they still won't leave."

"Don't you wanna save the bees, Ma?"

"Enough, Cam." She ran her palm down her face, stretching her skin as she groaned in disbelief. "Do I even *want* to know how you came across another dragon?"

With a shrug, Camaráin said, "You already *do* know."

Ma narrowed her eyes, then pressed her thumb and forefinger to the bridge of her nose. "You mean, all this time that smuggler and Lord Saibhir were accusing your sister of stealing multiple eggs from them, there actually *were* multiple eggs?"

"Yeah."

"Why didn't you *say* anything?"

"No one asked."

"Oh, for the love of..." Ma looked to the ceiling, which Cam knew she would do when she wanted to look to the heavens, but couldn't because the ceiling was blocking the view. "I don't have the words for that right now, young man. You realize that your sister could have—good *lord*, what is all over your bed, Cam?!" She finally saw the mess the hatchling had made.

"Um..." Camaráin took a glance at the dragon and held him out closer to Ma. "Well, him, mostly."

"Those were *clean* sheets, Camaráin."

"No they weren't."

"Hush." She tossed the bitten pie tin off to the side and buried her face in her hands. It had been a while since she had done that—Camaráin felt right at home after their long journey. A muffled scream erupted into Ma's hands as she shook her head. "This really...couldn't have waited, could it have? We...*just* returned from leaving Ailís in the Highlands. Don't tell me we now have to go *back* and leave you there, as well!"

A frown creased Cam's lips as he relaxed his arms, placing the dragon on the bed. While a warmth filled him at the thought of his new dragon, a pang of guilt struck him as he looked at his ma. "That won't happen, Ma," he assured her. "I'm not going anywhere." He hoped his firm stance and hands on hips was enough to instill confidence in her.

She looked up, her eyes red. "How can you be so sure? Did your sister think the same?"

"I never know *what* she's thinking half the time." He shrugged. "But I have a good feeling about this, is all. This time, it'll be different."

Ma looked unconvinced. If anything, it seemed like she expected to walk through the same story all over again.

That wasn't lost on Cam. "This is different," he said with a smile. With a glance at the dragon, he added, "Right?"

The dragon offered an inquisitive grunt and spread his wings in an approximation of a shrug.

"Good enough!" Cam exclaimed.

Rolling her eyes, Ma waved a dismissive hand and said, "Fine, fine. We're not throwing him a birthday party. I've had enough of those to last me a while."

Camaráin hesitated to remind her that it was *his* birthday tomorrow. There was always next year. "Then," he said, looking at the dragon again, "I can keep him?"

"Like I have a say in the matter." Ma sighed and shook her head. She muttered something under her breath about "being too *something* for this," but Camaráin didn't catch what she said. She seemed to be indicating she'd soon be off on one of her late-night adventures that left her sick come the morning. That usually happened when he and his sister pushed her buttons.

"Hurray!" Cam cheered. He skipped back to his bed and lifted the hatchling up again. "Well, how about it, Tinaeron? Are you ready for an adventure?"

Before the dragon could respond, Ma raised her eyebrow and asked, "'Tinaeron?'"

"What?" Camaráin inclined his head toward her with a frown. "That's what I decided to name him. I saw it in a book once. I think it means—"

"Can't you just give him a normal name like your sister did and make it easier for all of us?" Ma walked out of the room in a huff. After a moment's silence, the front door slammed shut.

Camaráin chewed at his bottom lip and muttered, "I'll give *you* a normal name," in a mocking tone. After a sharp breath, he looked back at the dragon briefly known as Tinaeron and asked, "You wanna just be called Brían or something?"

Brían the dragon raised his wings in mock triumph.

Chapter Two

Two weeks passed without incident, which Camaráin hoped to be able to rub in his sister's face one day.

The days went by with a steady routine: the lad would wake up, Brían often nestled in the crook of his arm, the heat from the hatchling's scales enough to keep Camaráin warm throughout the night. Ma would cook breakfast, which Cam would share with Brían, much to Ma's chagrin and annoyed acceptance, and the boy and his dragon would find their way over to the nearest chair. Brían had quickly taken a vested interest in whatever Camaráin opted to read.

Today was no different. As Camaráin leaned back in the large reading chair in the corner of the main room, wooden legs creaking, he surveyed his surroundings. Rays of sunlight beamed in through the window, the first time he had seen the sun south of the Highlands in what felt like ages. Breadcrumbs still peppered the dining table, Ma focused instead on cleaning the pans in the washbasin next to the stove at the opposite end of the room. An aroma of eggs, soda bread, and fresh butter lingered throughout the house.

Camaráin took in the words of his book in silence, Brían perched atop his shoulder with much the same focus.

And...that was it. Quiet. Peace.

Stopping his read mid-sentence, Camaráin could not help but sigh. Things had been much more interesting when Pilib hatched for Ailís. He looked at Brían from the corner of his eye, and even the dragon appeared to shrug his shoulders.

He assumed his ma was happy for the fact. After all, he *did* promise her that this would be different, that things would not proceed the same as they had for his sister. What that would entail, though, he had no idea.

When a knock at the door resounded through the house, he couldn't help but perk up. On instinct, he lifted and dropped his shoulder to urge the dragon off. "Brían," he hissed in as soft a voice as he could manage. "You need to hide right—"

"It's fine, Cam," Ma said without glancing toward him. She dropped the pan she had been working on in the washbasin and wiped her wet hands against her apron.

Camaráin was surprised at who stood on the other side when Ma opened the door.

"Well, then, good morning to you, too," Áine said with a smile. The former Draconic Priest crossed the threshold at Ma's invitation, a renewed spring in her step with which Camaráin was unfamiliar. A glimmer of light seemed to shine in her bright blue eyes, and her dark brown hair bounced at shoulder's length. When he had met her at his uncle's cottage in the Crann Woods, it had been clear the visit was against her will, and the remainder of the journey had left her with an expression of exhaustion.

But now? There was cheer that Camaráin could not help but think he played an active part in restoring. Or, perhaps not as active a part as his sister played. Or Pilib. Or journeying to the

Draconic Highlands. Or the great dragon Ollepheist launching both her former colleague (or, mortal enemy) and the High Inquisitor into the sea. But, at the least, Camaráin could say he played *a* part in the whole kit and caboodle.

Ma closed the front door and greeted Áine with a hug. "It's good to see you."

"You too, Máirín," Áine responded. She turned to look at Camaráin—or, perhaps more specifically, the dragon still perched atop his shoulder. "I did say I'd be happy to see you again when the time presented itself, didn't I, Cam? I just didn't think it'd happen so quickly."

Camaráin was too surprised at Áine's arrival to respond with much of anything, but he still nudged the dragon off his shoulder to hold him up toward her. "This is...Brían. He, um...he likes books?"

Brían held his head high with a dignified air.

Áine chuckled. "Well, I'm sure you two are getting along famously. Does he have a favorite yet?"

"Um...I don't know," Cam said. "I think he just likes looking at the pages. When there are pictures of faeries, he really perks up. But it's not like he can talk, so he can't tell me."

"Of course not. I'm sure he will in no time, though." There was hesitation in Áine's words as though she was considering what he said. A smile quickly returned to her face. "The Inquisition may not be a bother anymore, but you two are keeping each other safe, aren't you?"

"Yes, ma'am."

"Don't call me 'ma'am.' I'm not that old. But good." She reached out and tussled his hair.

Camaráin grimaced and ducked out of the way, failing to

stifle a laugh. Though he smiled at the Priest, he could not deny that her question gave him pause. He looked at Brían and knew, without a second thought, he'd always protect him. But the dragon seemed to regard him with some degree of disinterest. It was hard not to be curious.

"Cam," Ma said, breaking the silence. She gestured toward their guest. "Would you mind taking Brían and your book to your room? Áine and I need to talk for a little bit."

"We're talking *now*, though," Camaráin said with a bit of cheek.

"*Camaráin.*"

"Okay, Ma." He did as he was bid and grabbed his book from his chair and brought Brían to his room. He closed the door and leaped atop his bed, leaning against the wall as he opened the book back up. The dragon found his way under the book and blocked Cam's view of the words.

Not like Cam had any intention of actually reading. He had always been fascinated with how Ma knew when he and Ailís would try and sneak some pie. As he pressed his ear against the wall, he was reminded by how near the voices in the other room were and that the walls were paper-thin. He could practically shove his head through and emerge from the other side. He had no plans to actually do that. Not again, anyway.

"I can see why you took the time to write, Mairín," he heard Áine say.

"You can tell just by saying two words to him?"

"I said a lot more than just two words."

"*Áine.*"

"What can I say? The boy's snark is contagious."

"I think I liked you better when you were brooding and

wanting nothing to do with my brother."

"Well, I'm still half that, anyway."

Ma let loose an exasperated sigh. Maybe Camaráin would get along with Áine after all.

"Regardless," Áine continued, "I thought you'd be relieved that he's not exhibiting anything indicative of a Bond after everything that happened with Ailís."

"I am, truthfully," Ma said with some hesitation. She seemed to be shuffling in place. "It's just...should we be concerned? For Ailís, it was almost instant after Pilib hatched. It's been over two weeks and Cam hasn't shown a hint of it. No talk of dreams, no strange sensations, no magic, no nothing."

"Mairín, it's probably a good thing an eight-year-old isn't able to call fire."

"Hence why I'm relieved. But I'm not blind to the fact Cam might be frustrated by it."

"Little brothers are always getting jealous of their big sisters."

"Brothers and sisters don't usually have competitions over who can do the coolest things with their dragons."

"Well, not anymore, anyway."

"As if we need another thing."

Camaráin looked down at Brían, the dragon's focus still squarely on the contents of the book. He ran his hand along the warm scales and then stared at his hand. He flexed his fingers, hoping to feel...something. Anything resembling the connection Ailís felt with Pilib. But there was nothing. Brían craned his head around to look at Camaráin, and once again moved his shoulders in an approximation of a shrug. One had to wonder if the hatchling had any interest in such a competition with Pilib.

"You must have an idea, though, right?" Ma asked. "How long

it normally takes for these Bonded abilities to...I don't know, manifest? Happen? Appear out of thin air when a weird man in the woods tries to steal your dragon?"

"Mairín, until a few weeks ago, I never had to give a second thought to any of this," Áine said. "Honestly, I couldn't tell you one way or the other."

"Surely, there's someone you could ask, yes?"

"Yeah, sure, I'll just get in touch with the other Draconic Priests real quick."

"You don't have to be sarcastic, Áine."

The conversation carried on in much the same manner, but Camaráin tuned it out. He closed his book and looked at Brían, holding the dragon up to eye level. "There's nothing to worry about, right, Brían?"

The dragon grumbled non-affirmingly.

"Well, we'll figure it out together. Maybe there's something about it in this book, huh? Let's get to it."

Camaráin picked his copy of *Upscaled: The Official Novelization of the Novel* back up and dove back into its contents. A few pages in, though, and he felt like he knew it all already.

Chapter Three

I t was easy to feel a bit disappointed after finishing the book. Camaráin closed the book after what felt like a blink, and couldn't help but shake his head after reading two hundred pages of things he already knew about. The exile of the dragons beyond the Cliffs of Ard, what a Bond entails between a human and hatchling, the general incompetence of the Inquisition—the book may as well have been written by his uncle Iósaf.

Even Brían huffed with annoyance once the book was closed.

Camaráin ran his hand along the back of the dragon's head. "I know, I'm sorry. I wish there was more about you in it, too."

The hatchling tilted his head up and unfurled his wings in an approximation of a sneer.

"Well, it's not *my* fault! Who knows how long ago this was written?"

Brían grumbled again, dipping his head low.

"Well, that's good for you, then. You can write the next one." Camaráin had no idea what the dragon was saying, if anything.

Tossing the book aside, he turned his attention back to the main room. Whatever discussion Ma and Áine had been having had long since faded, and they seemed to be enjoying idle chit-chat. An enchanting aroma wafted in through the slits of the door. Camaráin had no idea how he had missed baked goods.

He held Brían up to eye level and asked, "Do you want some pie?" He grinned.

His excitement was not reciprocated. The dragon merely grunted in deference.

"Hmph. You're no fun." Cam placed Brían atop his shoulder and made for the door, the disappointment of his fruitless search for answers superseded by the promise of pie.

His heart sank only further when he made his way into the main room to find the pie tin was empty. Ma and Áine sat at the table, eyeing him as he walked in, their conversation ended in an instant. A moment of mirth was visible upon Áine's face, but it vanished in the same instant. It took Cam all his willpower not to sink to his knees and curse the heavens.

Áine patted the corner of her mouth with a napkin. "Oh, my. *Now* he decides to emerge from his room." The plate in front of her was littered with small crumbs and a smear of cooked blackberries.

"Why didn't you tell me?" Camaráin asked with a shaking voice, his hands balled into tremoring fists.

"We did," Ma said. "Several times. We couldn't rouse you from your book."

"But how did you eat the pie so quickly?"

"Cam, it's been three hours."

He blinked with surprise. He peered out the window and saw the sun much lower than it had been when last he was out here. "Oh, oops." The dragon trilled in his ear with what sounded like amusement, and Camaráin stuck his tongue out at him. "Is there more? Or...can there be more? Please?"

Ma crossed her arms and glared at him with a stone face. "*Camaráin.*"

Her piercing eyes shrunk him down, and a chill ran up his spine. "Sorry, Ma," he said.

The room remained in stark silence, the tension dense to the point of being able to grab it. At least, until Áine burst into laughter.

Rolling her eyes, Ma shook her head at the woman. "Couldn't keep up the act for longer than a minute, could you?"

"Lord above, Mairín, you had *me* nervous," Áine said. She breathed a long sigh of relief. Pointing a thumb over her shoulder, she added, "The rest is in your ma's bedroom, Cam. Go grab it, would you?"

The jaunt to Cam's step returned and he very nearly ran through his ma's bedroom door. (Brían slapped the doorframe with his wing for good measure.) He paid little attention to the mess of sheets atop her bed and the unfolded laundry strewn about the floor, and eyed a second pie tin atop the dresser, mercifully full save for the two slices he assumed Ma and Áine ate already. With caution, he picked up the tin, still warm on the bottom but not so hot he couldn't touch it and brought it back to the dining table. He had to control himself to not sprint to grab a clean plate and fork.

After taking the first bite, Camaráin leaned his head back and hummed his approval. "Áine, you make the best pies," he said with a wide smile.

Ma raised her eyebrows. "Who's to say *I* didn't bake it, hmm?"

Cam slunk his shoulders again and sheepishly pointed toward Áine. "But...hers are just...I mean..."

Áine flashed her teeth with amusement. "Oh, stop torturing the poor boy, Mairín. You can't fault him for having a strong palate."

"I invite you into my home, and you upstage me with your baking." Ma's words indicated offense, but her body language spoke otherwise. She tried and failed to hide her smile.

While the adults had their mock argument, Camaráin devoured his slice but for one small bite. He held it up by his fork and let it hover in front of Brían's nose. "Last chance, Brían."

The dragon was hardly chomping at the bit. He turned his head and rested atop the boy's shoulder.

"Your loss." Camaráin let the last bite slide off the fork and into his mouth. "I guess he doesn't like pie as much as Pilib did, huh?"

"Very few dragons do, Cam," Áine said with a chuckle. She leaned back in her chair, arms crossed over her body. "I wouldn't think too much into it."

"What do you mean, 'don't think too much into it?'" Cam asked, crumbs flying from his mouth. He apologized and wiped his face with a napkin before his ma could scold him.

Ma threw her hands up in the air. "We only *pretend* we can't hear one another from the other room, don't we, Cam?"

No point in arguing against that. It didn't change the fact he felt guilty at overhearing the conversation.

"So, then," Áine said, clasping her hands atop the table, "I'm sure you have some questions to ask me."

Camaráin blinked and smacked his lips together. After licking a remnant of the pie out from the corner of his gums, he scratched the back of his head and said, "I don't know. Not really."

The eager smile that had been plastered across Áine's face vanished in an instant. "'Not really?'" she parroted. "What do you mean? I thought you'd have a million questions about your Bond with Brían...or lack thereof."

Ma nodded. "I can tell you're frustrated, Cam. Even if you don't admit it."

Scratching the underside of the dragon's chin, Camaráin considered the words. He also considered getting another slice of pie, but assumed Ma would get cross with him if he did, so he elected not to. He couldn't deny that it was irksome that there was no trace of a Bond with Brían whatsoever, not even something so simple as a dream. But whenever sleep took him these last two weeks, his dreams remained ever the same—filled mostly with reading in massive libraries or throwing food at his sister and getting away with it.

But as he looked at his ma, he knew that frustration didn't matter in the grand scheme of things. "It's okay, Ma. Isn't it? I said things would be different, right? So..." He glanced at his feet, dangling off the edge of the chair. "So, I don't want you to worry about anything, that's all." The dragon was growing heavy on his shoulder, and he nudged Brían into his lap instead, running his hand along the back of his neck. "And he's still here, anyway, so that's more than enough for now."

A half-smile creeped across Ma's lips, but she remained quiet.

Áine raised her hand to the side of her mouth to block her lips and whisper-yelled to Ma, "You're *sure* he's the eight-year-old?"

"Believe me, most days he does quite well to remind me." Ma's expression was stern as she looked back at Cam, but it still hid a grin.

A knock at the door diverted everyone's attention. After the previous knock heralded Áine's arrival, Camaráin was in no rush to hide Brían's presence while his ma answered the door.

Hence why he was startled when the door opened to reveal a tall slab of moving armor standing beyond the threshold, a scroll held in an outstretched hand.

"Inquisition Postal Service!" shouted a deep voice, though Camaráin saw neither a head nor a mouth accompanying the armor.

With a chuckle, Ma took the paper and looked up as far as her head would allow. "Good day to you, Eamon. Finally getting some work again?" Her amusement wasn't even thinly-veiled. The veil had been removed and thrown in the mud.

Gauntleted arms crossed over the armor's breastplate, and it was only then that Camaráin realized Eamon was standing within it. He was still a giant of a man—perhaps even taller since last he saw him a few weeks prior—and still filled out his armor well. Why he *remained* in the armor was a different matter entirely, but the sigil that once belonged to the Inquisition of the Priory of the Thrice-Dead Prophet—or was co-opted by the Inquisition, at any rate—had been covered on the breastplate by a slip of paper that read "MAIL!!"

"I'm happy to be employed again, that is true," Eamon called from above. "It has been difficult for we Inquisitors since the protests against our authority began and High Inquisitor Dónal disappeared."

"Hmm, what a shame," Ma said, already half-closing the

door.

"It is good to have coin in my pocket again," Eamon continued.

"I hadn't realized you received payment as an Inquisitor—I
thought it to be an appointment by the Priory."

"I *wasn't* paid. That's why it's good to have coin again."

"You weren't paid at all?"

"Nope."

"Hold on, how did you afford clothing?"

"You're looking at it?"

"Housing?"

"We all took turns sharing a room at the edge of the village."

"Food?"

"Usually nabbed some from houses while on inspection."

"Lord above, how did it take this long for people to rise
against you?"

Eamon shrugged. "You're asking the right questions, Mairín.
Hey! On the topic of the right questions, maybe you and I could
grab a—"

"Nope." Ma closed the door and walked back to the table.
Outside, it sounded like Eamon was continuing whatever "right
questions" before the sound of clinking armor fading into the
distance signaled his departure.

Camaráin eyed the scroll as his ma unfurled it. "What is it?
We never get mail!"

Scoffing, Ma said, "*You* never get mail. *I* get too much." She
read the paper in silence, her eyes darting back and forth as
she went line by line. As she finished, she clenched her eyes
shut and let loose a shaking breath.

"Mairín?" Áine asked, concern evident on her face. "Is

something the matter?"

Ma frowned and rapped the rolled paper against her palm. "Just my parents."

"Did something happen?"

"Huh? Oh, no, no, everything's fine." She looked at Camaráin with wide eyes and open hands and repeated, "Everything's *fine*. They just wrote to invite us down to visit, is all."

Camaráin's eyes lit up. "Granma and Granda's house? Yay!"

"Are they close?" Áine asked.

"Down in Beag, bit of a hike. It's been a while," Ma said.

"Oh, didn't realize they lived near the capital. I've not been to Mór in ages. I may feel a bit inclined to visit the libraries and—" Áine paused, eyeing Ma with renewed concern. "What is it?"

Planting her hands on her hips, Ma tossed the scroll on the table and sighed. "I've not had the chance to tell them...about Ailís. How she's off in the Highlands. With my brother. And a bunch of dragons. I'm not exactly looking forward to having that conversation."

Áine grunted in affirmation. She leaned back and crossed her arms, clicking her lips together. "Glad I don't have to do that."

"Thanks."

Camaráin, meanwhile, held Brían up and placed him on the table. "But I can show them Brían! I can show them a dragon!"

Ma's eyes nearly rolled into the back of her head. "I don't think that will help."

Brían turned his head as though he was offended.

Camaráin shrugged and muttered, "Not with that attitude, it won't."

Chapter Four

The bell tolled loud and proud throughout the cathedral. It always did, and in Una's opinion, it was far too loud and proud. Her ears still rang with the echoes of the tolls of two minutes past.

She sat in a rear pew, her eyes trained on the High Prior's sermon, as much as she could see him through the rows upon rows of people in front of her. What little sunlight that could burst through the heavy cloud cover trickled through the stained-glass windows as weak sunbeams. The altar stood tall in its extravagance, swathed in gold and reaching toward the painted ceiling some six stories above. It was Sunday, and so most of the population of Mór had arrived to receive the High Prior's sermon.

Or, more a lecture on whatever was on the man's mind. Una did not necessarily consider herself devout or well-versed in the Priory's teachings, but it was not lost on her that many of the "sermons" of the last few months were rants of what was presently giving the High Prior displeasure. Last month, he was yelling about clouds and invited the congregation to join him in shaking their fists at the sky later that afternoon, claiming they blocked Nóra from the Lord's light or some such. Previous to that, he tripped on a cobblestone and made a blithe jape about removing them from the streets of Mór and throwing them at the cobbler's house. People took him at his word, and none seemed to question that a shoemaker was not party to urban design.

Today, though?

"Selkies!" he shouted in a wavering voice, echoing throughout the crowd. The attendees gasped.

All except for Una, at any rate. Instead, she rested her forehead against her thumb and forefinger and muttered, "Good lord." He had just been speaking of green paint a moment ago, so why he decided to shout "Selkies!" was beyond her.

The High Prior raised his arms at his side, the wide sleeves of his robe wafting to the ground in an extravagant display of golden excess. "I speak earnest and true!" he proclaimed.

"You spoke the name of a creature that exists, so I guess that's not false," Una said under her breath.

"Ever vigilant must we remain in the pursuit and caution of the fae, and now is no exception! On our shores, a selkie has been spotted, wreaking havoc upon fair sailors who draw too near, and to unfair sailors who do not draw near enough. We must protect them all!"

The crowd raised their voices to the air, some putting a hand to their chests in shock, some crying out for help from above, and some hiding beneath the pew benches and bawling like babies. Only the bravest cowered in fear of something that was nowhere near them.

Una raised her head and craned an eyebrow. Every now and again, the Priory would suddenly remember they had a bone to pick with the fae. She never understood why, but it made her interests a pain to pursue.

"To that end," the High Prior continued, "I have elected to employ the services of the…um…what are you lot calling yourselves now?" He gestured toward someone in the front row, curling and uncurling his fingers to beckon them forward.

A man walked up to join the High Prior on the altar, clad in heavy black leathers, dark hair slicked back to a frame a heavily bearded face. He was of short and stocky build, but still managed to tower over the slim and slender frame of the High Prior. He spoke at a conversational volume with the old man, but not loud enough for Una to hear him.

Still, she could not help but groan. "Of course it's Robeárd. Everyone's favorite self-important blowhard."

The High Prior drew in a sharp breath. "You cannot call yourselves *that* now!"

Robeárd said something that did not carry over the crowd, but Una could read his lips well enough to tell he responded with something along the lines of, "Why not?"

"Because it's a stupid name!"

Another quiet remark from Robeárd.

"Ours is a sacred name, I'll have you know!"

Again, too quiet a retort.

"Yes, when *we* do so, it's good!" He turned his nose up and returned his attention to the crowd, clearing his throat. "At any rate, we have brought Robeárd and his band of…" He shuddered with disgust. "…*companions* to bring this selkie to heel and protect the fair citizens of Mór! The Priory shall always care for its flock!"

A round of applause and cheers rang out through the cathedral. Some jumped to their feet and started pumping their fists in the air. The High Prior took the opportunity to snap his fingers, summoning a small army of lower priors with collection baskets. Say one thing for the High Prior, say he knew how to work a crowd well enough to get them to leave too much money in the basket.

Una remained seated and quiet, gnawing at her lower lip as she squirmed in place. Her eyes did not leave Robeárd. "Sure hope they don't find that selkie," she muttered, crossing her arms. "I promised her I'd go dancing with her next week."

Chapter Five

Camaráin had never ridden in a horse-drawn carriage before. He hated it.

It wasn't long ago that his grandparents lived just a morning's walk away from Baile, but as they grew older, they professed a desire to move further south, which he had read was something old folks tended to do. He couldn't quite determine why—a glance outside the carriage would reveal the same green pastures and cloudy skies as existed further north. It just seemed an inconvenience for all parties involved.

Especially now that, instead of a morning jaunt, he was subjected to a three-day journey by carriage. Each bump in the road was another bruise on his bottom. The interior of the carriage stank of bodily odors, none of it his own. Ma had told him the driver slept there while they got to stay at roadside inns, and from the man's slick and sweaty appearance, it was easy to believe. Camaráin had also dropped a bowl of porridge at the outset of the journey and felt too embarrassed to raise the issue, and it had gone bad.

It was a miracle he hadn't gone mad from the boredom. He wished he had brought his book with him, though Ma warned that discussing the plot of *Scales and Tales for the Boys and*

Gæls was not something she wished to have with Granma and Granda around. It was a fair point—they were already due to be perplexed at Brían's presence. The dragon shared a mutual disinterest in the goings-on of the journey; neither the same rolling green hills of the previous day nor the overcast sky could rouse him from his slumber, which Camaráin could only assume was far more exciting.

A quiet journey through the Nóran countryside was just boring after the adventure he had had a few weeks prior.

The tedium was at last broken at midday when the driver called, "Land, ho!"

Ma huffed a breath. "We were always on land," she said.

Brían stretched his long neck and grunted out a yawn. Annoyance colored his eyes at being woken up, and he rested his head back along the rear of the carriage.

Peering his head out of the window, Camaráin's eyes lit up when signs of civilization finally revealed themselves to him. Beyond the hills of green and the plains of green and the greens of green sprung tall buildings crafted of elaborate stone, brick, and wood, wisps of smoke wafting out of smokestacks and reaching to the sky. Even at this distance, a pinprick on the horizon, it was a sight matched in extravagance only by the Draconic Highlands.

The village of Beag was visible from the opposite window and was smaller and much less impressive in stature. It had some regular houses and regular fields. "It just looks like Baile," Camaráin muttered.

"Aye, but much smaller!" shouted the driver.

"No one asked you," Ma said, crossing her arms.

"Smells better, too!"

Ma crinkled her nostrils. "Compared to...?"

The driver responded only with silence, his shoulders slumping. "Be quiet." He sounded upset, near on the verge of tears.

"Never insult a fragile man's home," Ma whispered, leaning closer to Camaráin. "Also, don't become a fragile man when you grow up."

"I didn't plan on it." The free real estate was tempting, though.

After another ten silent minutes navigating the downward slopes of the southern Nóran countryside, the carriage pulled up at the village mouth of Beag. Camaráin hopped out of the carriage, stowing Brían in his bag, and breathed deep the air. After the musty smells of the open road and confined carriage, it was invigorating smelling fresh air again. That the sea was so close created an aroma all the more enchanting.

The driver hopped down to the ground, patting the rump of the left-side horse and meeting the earth with a metallic thump. It had been easy to ignore while daydreaming in the carriage, but all the harder for Camaráin to ignore now the Inquisitor standing before him. Or, former Inquisitor, at any rate. This wasn't an Inquisitor with whom Camaráin was familiar, so it was likely he never patrolled around Baile. The man stood at barely five feet tall, and his armor had the appearance of being fitted for someone at least a foot taller. He looked every bit the child trying on his father's clothing. He planted his gauntleted hands on his hips and flashed a wide smile at Ma as she alighted.

Ma rolled her eyes as she looked at him.

"Thank you for riding with Inquisition Transit!" the driver

said.

"Uh-huh," Ma grunted.

He held out an empty hand, his gauntlet sliding off to reveal a sweaty palm. "I believe a tip is customary."

"Air out the cabin before taking on a new customer."

He blinked in confusion.

"There's your tip."

Kicking at a pebble, the driver questioned, "A new customer...?"

Ma grasped Camaráin by the shoulder and pulled him alongside her, walking past the driver. "Come along now, Cam."

Brían poked his head out of the bag and squawked out his equivalent to a laugh at the driver's expense.

Ma chuckled and shook her head, though Camaráin did not understand why. The workings of commerce were beyond him, given the only book he had read on the subject was the book Uncle Iósaf had on how to commit tax fraud and get away with it.

They walked through the paved dirt roads of Beag, and up close, Camaráin was impressed at how much it *did* look like Baile. Granted, the pathways weren't muddy, and it didn't smell like mystery dung, and it wasn't too loud, and it looked like there were primarily residents of an older age, and the ocean could be seen at the crest of a hill, but beyond all that, it was just like Baile. It had...houses. Just like Baile. He felt right at home.

A small house loomed at a crossroad, separated from the rest of the near-identical homes. A small wooden fence enclosed a front yard with verdant green grass and a tree stump with a hand-axe lodged into it. Planters hung from the front windows, which had blinders blocking the interior, and a red wooden door caught the eye.

Ma drew a breath as she approached, her fingers nervously digging into Camaráin's shoulders.

"Ma, that hurts," he said with a whimper.

She drew her hand back and made to knock the door.

Before her knuckles met the wood, the door swung open, and she instead knocked on her father's face. It didn't resound the same way a door would.

"You always did have a knack for knowing when we'd be arriving."

"Yes, it's called 'looking out the window,'" Granda said. "Can you please stop knocking on my face?"

"Huh?" Ma had continued to lightly knock on Granda's nose, but finally stopped. "Oh, right, sorry. Hi, Da." She gave him a hug.

Granda reciprocated, patting her on the back of the head. "Good to see you." He looked over her shoulder and eyed Camaráin with a smile. "And look at you, little man, you've gotten so big!"

It had been some time since Camaráin had last seen his grandparents. Granda had gained some more grays and whites in his hair and goatee, but he looked slimmer than when Camaráin last saw him. He had apparently taken up running as a hobby, which Camaráin was unaware was a thing people actually did. It didn't sound fun. As ever, though, his cheeks puffed out red as he cast a wide smile toward his grandson. "Hi, Granda," Camaráin said, skipping over to embrace him and ignoring the rustling at his hip.

At Camaráin's grip, Granda feigned physical pain. However,

at his own kneeling, he did not feign any pain, so it evened out. He grunted as he rose back to his feet and winced at the effort, but maintained the smile, nonetheless. At least, until he noticed it was only the two of them. "Mairín?" he asked. "Where is Ail—wait, what is *that?*" He pointed at something.

Camaráin looked down and saw Brían's head was poking out of his bag. "Oh. This is...my dragon?" he said.

"What?" Granda looked at Brían and only a slight amount of surprise colored his face. "Huh. Didn't expect that. But, no, I mean, what is *that?*" He pointed again.

Ma and Camaráin turned around to see their driver at the fence's opening, his hands tucked into his armor's pockets. The Inquisitors were always excited that their armor had pockets, despite the lack of utility for them.

"Oh, that's our carriage driver," Ma said brusquely before narrowing her eyes at him. "Did you need something?"

"Um..." the driver looked at the ground and kicked at another rock. "You wouldn't happen to know where I can get a horse, do you? Some teenagers took mine."

Granda leaned in close and whispered to Ma, loud enough for Camaráin to hear, "Is this not an Inquisitor?"

"A *lot* has happened up north. I'll fill you in later," Ma whispered in response. "It was the best bargain to get down here. He didn't realize we were supposed to pay him with money."

"What did you pay him with?"

"Nothing. It was a great bargain."

Granda scoffed and shook his head at the ex-Inquisitor. "Come on, you two. Or three. Let's head inside. Granma's waiting."

"Oh, thank you, sir!" the driver exclaimed, taking an excited step forward.

"I wasn't talking to you," Granda retorted, gesturing instead toward Ma, Camaráin, and Brían. The door shut behind the trio as they heard a disappointed groan from behind.

Camaráin surveyed the house's interior—it was smaller than the home they previously owned, but he supposed they needed less space nowadays. A living room, bedroom, and kitchen were the only rooms he could see, and each was arrayed with minimal furniture and maximum natural light—at least, it would have been, had the blinds not been drawn. He was curious about that, and about the closed door at the other end of the living room.

Before he could investigate further, though, a small woman with shoulder length brown hair emerged from the kitchen, a pair of rectangular spectacles sliding down the bridge of her nose. A smile stretched from ear to ear as she looked at her new arrivals.

"Granma!" Camaráin exclaimed, rushing to her and nearly plowing her over.

"Oh! Good to see you, too, Cam," she said, stifling a chuckle.

Again, Brían scurried about from within Camaráin's bag, but this time slithered out enough to fall. The dragon scampered across the floor and made his way to the couch, where he immediately lounged. He rested his back against the couch, spread-eagled, and it seemed he had already fallen asleep by the way his head lolled.

Granma hummed in confusion at the sight, holding up a finger and asking, "Mairín, where's Ailís?"

Ma gestured toward the sleeping dragon on the couch. "You don't wanna...ask about that?"

"Huh? Oh, this isn't the first time one of you has brought home a strange pet." Granma chuckled. "Do you remember that time your brother tried to bring a lanternshark inside? Always resourceful and fearless, that one. And a little dumb."

"I don't even know how he got it—they're not from this area. No idea how he kept it alive, either. We were days away from the water."

"Ah, that boy," Granma said with a contented sigh. The contentedness disappeared when Granda cleared his throat and raised an eyebrow. "Oh, right. Where's my granddaughter?"

Ma leaned against the wall and crossed her arms, lowering her head into her chest. "That's a long story. *Right, Cam?*" Her eyes burrowed a hole in Camaráin's chest.

He slunk to hide behind Granma, which was hard since he was already taller than her.

After a moment's silence, Ma detailed everything that had happened over the last few weeks: the dragons being discovered; Ailís awakening to strange abilities; the pursuit of the smuggler, Inquisition, and Lord Saibhir; their reunion with Iósaf; and, ultimately, leaving Ailís and Iósaf in the Draconic Highlands so the girl could train in the art of the Bond. Camaráin found it strange how similar those proceedings were to when he read *Upscaled: The Official Novelization of the Novel* the other day.

"...and, much to my...I still haven't decided on an emotion, but as you can see, we've another dragon in our midst," Ma concluded. "At least there hasn't been a need to haul ourselves back up north again."

Camaráin looked at his feet. He still couldn't feel anything from Brían.

Granma and Granda leaned back on the couch, having sat there at the beginning of the story. The dragon was not once roused from his slumber. They regarded each other in silence after Ma finished, though Granma's attention seemed to be elsewhere.

"Well," she said, "I suppose she had to leave the nest eventually, right?"

"Aindréa," Granda said in a low voice. "She's eleven years old. And she's by herself."

"She has Iósaf with her."

Granda raised an eyebrow.

"Okay, fair point. The dragons will look after her, then."

Ma shifted against the wall. "You seem...unbothered by the whole 'dragons' thing."

Granma reached over and scratched Brían under the chin. The dragon seemed to smile at her touch. Camaráin frowned at the sight.

"Well, yes," Granma said. "The Inquisition never bothered down here, so dragons were never a thing to be feared."

"Why didn't they come down here?" Camaráin asked.

"From what I heard, Mór was too large for them to walk around," Granda said.

"Too few people?"

"No, too lazy."

Ma grunted. "That sounds about right."

A distant smile remained on Granma's face as she scratched at Brían's chin, even though the dragon remained asleep. Her gaze still drifted.

"Granma?" Camaráin asked. "What's wrong? You've been looking at that door for a while." He pointed toward the closed door at the back of the living room.

Offering a questioning look to her husband, Granma asked, "Should we ask them?"

"Eventually, they're going to need to use the bathroom," Granda responded. "*I* still haven't gotten to use it. It's been *three days*, Aindréa."

"Padraig, too much information."

"Da, eww." Ma uncurled her tongue in disgust. She gestured toward her parents with a shrug. "What is it?"

Tapping her fingertips nervously, Granma gritted her teeth and said, "We sort of...had another reason for asking you down here." She inclined her head toward the closed door. "Padraig, if you wouldn't mind."

Shaking his head with annoyance, Granda walked over to the door and opened it wide.

Camaráin heard a vile string of gibberish and loud stomping the moment it opened. He craned his head around the corner, and his eyes opened wide. "I didn't expect to see one of them again any time soon," he murmured.

"Tell me," Granma said. "What do you two know about gnomes?"

Chapter Six

"Hah, he's just like Adhamh!" Camaráin exclaimed.

"Ugh, he's just like Adhamh," Ma groaned.

Standing in the bathroom atop the chamber pot, the gnome flared his nostrils with clear annoyance and probable anger. His beady eyes were barely visible behind a thick wall of bushy grey eyebrows, a long beard of the same color stopping at his waist. Whether he was wearing a shirt, Camaráin could not tell. His hat was discarded, revealing a bald circle atop his head with thin wisps of long hair falling down his cheeks. Beads of sweat trickled down his forehead, and it stank.

Little wonder the gnome began to hurl a string of angry grunts in the fae tongue that Camaráin could only assume was "not kind enough for his ears."

"Seems we interrupted something," Ma said.

Granda hung his head and sighed with defeat. "No. It's just...always like this. I think he's holding us hostage for food."

Ma leaned in close to Camaráin and whispered, "That sounds familiar."

"Oh!" Granma perked right up. "So you *do* know a thing or two about gnomes."

"Not gnomes," Ma said, rolling her eyes. "Just obnoxious

younger brothers."

Granma planted her hands on her hips. "Camaráin! Have you been stealing food from your sister again?"

Feeling betrayal in his heart, Camaráin shot his eyes toward his ma. "Hey! I've never done that to Ailís! Why would you—"

"I'm talking about your uncle, Cam." Ma craned her eyebrow.

"Oh, right."

"What?" Granda leaned in close.

Ma chuckled. "I mean, does it surprise you?"

"Does what surprise me?"

Granma sighed and shook her head. "Close the door, Padraig." The gnome continued to (maybe) berate the family with (maybe) foul language.

The bathroom door shut, the gnomish shouts muted, to which Camaráin could only groan his disappointment. He felt he was close to a breakthrough of deciphering the gnomish language based on his "interactions" with Adhamh and his past skimming of Uncle Iósaf's enlightening read, *#%$&!: Angry Gnomish for Kind People*, and just needed more time listening to this fellow, but maybe another time.

"Now then," Granda continued, moving farther away from the door, and the gnome behind it. "What's this about a bundle?"

"I said nothing about a bundle, Da," Ma said.

"Sorry, old ears."

"Uncle Iósaf was living with a gnome!" Camaráin said.

"'Living with' is one way to put it," Ma muttered. "More like mooching off a gnome."

"But he said he won the house in a game of tic-tac-toe!"

Granda massaged the bridge of his nose with his forefingers.

"You know what, maybe we don't *need* to know all the details."

"Probably less infuriating that way," Ma agreed.

"It wasn't all bad, though," Camaráin said. He smiled to himself, paying little heed to the adults staring at him, waiting for him to continue the thought. He did not continue the thought.

"...and?" Ma prompted. "Do you have an example?"

Camaráin shrugged. "Adhamh chased those brigands away."

Ma opened her mouth as though to disagree, but she stopped herself and nodded. "I suppose there is *that*."

Granma glanced across the room. "Well, Padraig, I guess if we ever run into brigands, we can make use of him."

Granda didn't look amused.

"More to the point," Ma said, "what's a gnome doing this far south to begin with? Everything that I've read about them—"

"That *I've* read about them," Camaráin corrected.

"Hush. According to the Priory, the fae are only supposed to be in the Crann Woods. Why are they so close to the capital?"

"What are you talking about?" Granda said. "They've always been this far south."

Ma seemed taken aback. "What? But all the books about them say—"

"Don't believe everything you read in a book. Anyone can lie."

"Yeah!" Camaráin exclaimed. "Wasn't that the point of our last adventure? The Inquisition lied about the dragons. Look at Brían! Does he look evil?"

He pointed at the dragon, who still reclined on the couch, head craned all the way back, a mighty snore loosed from his mouth. It felt strong enough to shake the foundations of the house. His hind leg kicked at the air—it appeared as though he was having an eventful dream. Or he was just a violent sleeper. After the number of late-night kicks to the spine he'd received over the last few weeks, Camaráin still wasn't sure of which.

"I suppose that depends on what he's dreaming about," Ma deadpanned. "It was easier to tell with Pilib."

A point of disagreement was hard to find for Camaráin, so he remained quiet.

"Anyway," Granda continued, ignoring the pounding at the bathroom door, "there lies south of Mór a small grove where creatures of the fae dwell. Or perhaps hiding—the way the Priory keeps them under wraps, I'm not inclined one way or the other."

"The Priory keeps them under wraps?" Camaráin asked. "Why?"

A massive thud on the other side of the bathroom door resounded through the house, followed by another series of muted angry ramblings.

"Never mind, I think I understand why." Even after emerging from the Crann Woods unscathed by its fae denizens, the idea of more fae creatures lurking nearby gave Camaráin the heebie-jeebies. The angry and violent gnome was fine, though.

"More importantly," Ma added, "*how* would the Priory keep it all under wraps? Do folks around here just...*not* go in the woods?"

"Well, you know what they say," Granda said. "Live in the big city and you'll never see an inch of nature again."

"Nobody says that, Da."

"They will, I'm working on it."

The pounding at the door persisted in the background. On the couch, Brían's head lolled and his eyes began to flitter open.

A loud grunt escaped his mouth. He seemed quite annoyed at being woken up, despite having slept for most of the day. (Kids, right?)

"What your father was probably going to get to," Granma said, stepping forward to mercifully put the conversation back on track, "is that the Priory has taken to...well, no need to sugarcoat it. Hunting the fae for sport."

Camaráin's eyes widened. He didn't know what that meant, but he didn't like sports, so he probably wouldn't have been a fan of hunting for it.

"So, that gnome," Ma said, pointing to the still-pounded door. "He found his way here after escaping one of the Priory's hunts?"

Scoffing, Granda stared at the bathroom with what looked to be disbelief. "Him? I don't know. We just came home one day and he was in here. We don't know how. He was lounging on the coffee table like he owned the place."

"Sounds like Uncle Iósaf," Camaráin said.

"Different story, Cam, different story," Ma chided. "You sure you locked the door?"

"Positive," Granda affirmed.

"Think he slipped down the chimney?"

"Does he look like he gave us gifts?"

"Why was he sleeping on the table instead of the couch?"

"Do I look like I understand gnomes?"

"Why don't you ask him if he was part of a hunt?"

"Sure, I'll get *right* on that, Mairín. Just as soon as I learn to speak freaky-deaky angry gnome."

"Fae," Camaráin corrected.

"Hush," Ma and Granda said simultaneously.

Placing her hands on her hips, Granma hummed to herself and looked at the door. "Honestly, though, I can't see *him* being hunted by the Priory, can you?"

One more slam, and the door fell off its hinges. The gnome launched himself out of the bathroom and started jumping in place in the middle of the room, causing all sorts of a ruckus with his presumed foul language and clear foul breath.

"No, I cannot," Ma said, rolling her eyes. "Honestly, I'd feel worse for the Priory."

"What about crying peas?" Granda asked over the din of the gnome's shouting.

"*Priory!*" Ma shouted.

"*Me, Myself, and Irene?*" Granda "repeated."

An angry, frustrated roar sounded from the other side of the room. Camaráin looked to see Brían hunched over, ready to pounce, his eyes still flittering to focus, steam near about wafting from his nostrils.

It was the loudest he had ever heard a dragon roar. Which, given this was the *only* time he had heard an earnest roar from a dragon, and Brían sounded closer to a housecat in the attempt...well, at least it still won by default.

Baby's first roar aside, Brían was angry to have been woken up. He leapt off the couch, ready to release the hottest tantrum the people of Nóra had ever heard.

"I liked it better when he was asleep," Camaráin said.

Chapter Seven

The room burst into a flurry of movement as everyone took their stations in anticipation for what was to come. In the moments it took Brían to land on the ground, each embarked on their own journeys.

Granma grabbed the nearest chair and raised it high to level against whoever struck the first blow, because no one was going to beat her to the second blow.

Ma took two steps backward and rolled her eyes, wanting nothing to do with the proceedings. She half-turned toward the door.

Granda saw the opportunity to finally use the bathroom and rushed in, locking it behind him.

And Camaráin dropped to a crouched position, arms outstretched, ready to charge whenever needed. He based the stance off of something he read in *The Inquisitor's Guide to Fighting When You Leave Your Sword at the Dry Cleaner's*, though he was unsure of the proper use-case for the stance he had assumed. Tough to know when the book was all pictures and no explanations.

But for all the chaos while Brían remained aloft, when he came aground, it was entirely anticlimactic. Nothing had happened. For all the forward momentum Camaráin had carried himself with, the need not to lurch forward sent him plummeting face-first into the ground instead.

When he looked up, Granma still held a shaking chair high over her head, Ma was halfway out the door, a relieved sigh could be heard in the bathroom, and Brían and the gnome were regarding one another with what looked to be...familiarity.

The anger in the gnome's tone, mannerisms, body language, face—well, everything, really—vanished, and he seemed quite taken with the dragon. Camaráin could not help but feel confused. Concluding that every gnome in Nóra was the same as Adhamh, he had expected this fellow to want little at all to do with the hatchling. After all, Adhamh could not be bothered with Pilib during their encounter in the Crann Woods. (Granted, Adhamh could not be bothered with *anybody*, but that was beside the point.)

Instead, the gnome knelt beside Brían, extending a stubby arm toward him, brushing the length of his scaled neck with his hand. Words escaped his lips in a soft tone, and for once, Camaráin got the impression of a gnome speaking words that very well could have been for his ears. Part of him, though, still expected them to be quite foul but said in a much gentler tone.

And for Brían's part, the dragon greeted the gnome as he would an old friend...which made no sense whatsoever. Camaráin was his only friend, and after those first days, the boy felt Brían did not think of him as much of a friend at all. But here he was, looking at the gnome with none of the annoyance or mockery he often exhibited toward Camaráin, and instead trilled with the same friendliness and good humor Pilib would show Ailís. He seemed relaxed, content, his shoulders no longer tense and his wings furled against his frame.

If there was ever a time for Brían to say his first words, Camaráin would have gladly welcomed them.

"Well," Ma said, huffing a surprised breath as she closed the door and re-entered the living room. "That's not something you see every day."

"Ma, we never saw a dragon or a gnome until three weeks ago," Camaráin remarked.

"I know. That's why I said it's not something you see every day."

"Can I put the chair down?" Granma asked, already dropping the chair with a loud clang. "Okay, thanks."

"Does this make any sense to you?" Camaráin asked, looking at Ma. He furrowed his brow, feeling a pang of frustration and jealousy.

"Cam, none of this made sense even when there was *only* a dragon."

Crossing his arms with a harumph, Camaráin watched the newly-found lifelong friends enjoying one another's company without a care for anyone else in the room. Even as he waved his hands at Brían, the dragon's attention was paid solely to the gnome, and whatever kind and/or insulting words he was sharing with the dragon. Camaráin shut his eyes, humming to himself, trying to picture something, *anything*, from one of the books on dragons back home or the books in Uncle Iósaf's library, or even anything the Inquisition had to say on the fae.

"Cam?" Ma asked, inclining her head toward him. "Is everything okay?"

It was hard to deign that with a response. He already was exhibiting none of the Bonded magic that he expected he should have had by now. He had no connection with Brían despite being the one to carry his egg until hatching. Now, he could only ask why a dragon would have any relations with a gnome to begin with. He gasped with realization. "Do you think Brían is part-gnome?"

Ma gestured toward the dragon. "Cam. Look at him. What part of him looks like a gnome?"

Camaráin shrugged. "The attitude?"

"Fair."

The bathroom door swung open, and Granda emerged, hiking his trousers back up to his waist and sighing with relief. "Oh, good," he said. "The gnome found a friend. Why didn't we get a dragon earlier?"

With a deep frown, Camaráin turned away from the sight. "It doesn't make any sense. Why would he want to be friends with a gnome before me, anyway?"

Granda continued walking the length of the room before planting himself on the couch. A satisfied smile at the long-awaited silence stretched across his lips. "Who knows? The fae are strange folk. I heard there're scholars in Mór, so I'd assume they're even stranger. They'd probably eat this stuff up."

The thought lifted Camaráin's spirits, and he looked at Ma with wide eyes. "We can go to the capital?"

Ma flashed a glance at Granda. "Are you sure, Da? Someone could explain...whatever this is?" She held out a hand to the gnome and the dragon, who were already creating a secret handshake.

"Sure, I'm sure." He was not sure.

Camaráin hopped in place with excitement. "What are we

waiting for, then? Let's go!"

Granda leaned back on the couch with his fingers interlinked behind his head. "Ah, peace and quiet."

"You know the dragon is going with them, right, Padraig?" Granma said.

"And if the Priory is hunting fae, the gnome must stay here," Ma added.

The smile vanished from Granda's face. "Easy come and easy go." With a huff, he leaned forward, resting his arms atop his knees. "Then, will you show them around Mór, Aindréa?"

Camaráin inclined his head as he interrupted the secret handshake to put Brían atop his shoulder. The gnome was already growling. "You're not coming with us, Granda?"

Granda shook his head. "Oh, no. The last time I left *him* alone—" He pointed an accusatory finger at the gnome. "—the couch exploded."

The room went quiet, save for the gnome, who blew a raspberry at Granda and retreated back into the bathroom.

Noting that everyone's eyes lingered on the intact couch, Granda then added, "Well, it got better."

Granma did not seem inclined to share the story in full. She walked toward the door with a sigh and said, "Let's go, kids."

Camaráin really wanted to know the story.

Chapter Eight

A gentle sea breeze greeted Camaráin as he stepped outside, the air rich with the smell of salt. That a small village could manage not to smell like dung was still a foreign concept to him, and he was unsure whether he preferred the more pleasant aroma or would have rather returned to the devil he knew.

Ma followed, and Granma behind her, the tension thick inside the house as the war between Granda and the gnome seemed about to erupt once more. It reminded Camaráin of a book he read when he was younger called *Granda and the Gnome: A Tale of Peace, Love, and Other Such Nonsense*. It was only now he realized the book was likely a parody.

Regardless of the realism of the book, Granma closed the door with gritted teeth and slowly backed away, murmuring to herself, "We'll just hope the house is still standing when we return, won't we?"

Camaráin responded with a cheerful nod whilst Ma groaned and turned away, a letter visible in her hand. Though he had seen her writing it while they were readying themselves to set out, Camaráin didn't think to ask of its contents.

He followed after her as she walked toward a fellow in thick plate armor who looked lost, bored, or some combination of the two. On instinct, he nudged Brían off his shoulder, but the dragon reacted with indifference and remained atop, flashing a sneer at the interior to Camaráin's bag. The boy brought it up to his nose, took a whiff, and grimaced. "Okay, fair enough, Brían," he said. He had no idea how the stench of rotted fish got in there—or for how long it was there—but when all else failed, he defaulted to blaming his sister.

So lost in his reflections of his bag's poor self-care habits that he was startled to hear Ma shout, "You there!"

A man in Inquisitor armor turned to face them, his eyes flaring at the sight of Brían, but his lip curling downward at the remembrance that the Inquisition no longer served much of a purpose. "Yes, ma'am? How can I help you?" Even without the look of dejection on his face, he bore depressing features: sunken eyes with dark bags underneath, droopy cheeks that gave the impression of a permanent frown, and red eyes with tears streaming down that might have just been allergies, but could also possibly genuine tears. Camaráin was not inclined to inquire further.

Ma held up the letter as she continued her approach. "I have a letter to be delivered!"

He furrowed his brow. "Do I look like a postman, ma'am?"

"Are you anything *else* these days?" She pointed at his breastplate. "You've even painted 'MAIL' on your armor."

Head hanging low, he muttered, "Okay, ma'am." He held open an empty palm, and grimaced as the letter was shoved into it.

"Good." Ma took a step back and crossed her arms. "I want you to deliver this to a woman in the Crann Woods by the name of Áine. When you find a house with an angry gnome threatening to smack you over the head with your own gauntlet, go to the next house over."

The Notquisitor's eyes widened, two simultaneous complaints emerging from his mouth at once: "Crann—I can't—are so—another gnome—far away—so scary!"

"Not a clue what you said there, but get moving."

With a defeated sigh, the man turned around and said, "Yes, ma'am." Even his armor clanked with sadness as he disappeared around the bend.

Camaráin walked up beside his ma. "You wrote to Áine?"

Ma nodded, still sneering at the man long after he was out of view. "I figured it couldn't hurt to ask of her expertise with the fae, having lived amongst them for so long. And if she's able to come down here to Beag, then all the better."

"She'll be mad that she didn't get to finish her puzzle."

"Well, she'll be madder if she didn't get to meet the dragon who's part gnome."

Camaráin's eyes lit up. "You mean you *do* think Brían is part gnome?"

Ma scoffed. "No, but I needed to write *something* to convince her to travel down this way." She smirked, sharing a glance with the dragon, and then looked past Camaráin. "Shall we be off to Mór, then, Ma?"

"What a strange day," Granma muttered, shuffling past them.

When Camaráin had seen the Cliffs of Ard, and the Draconic Highlands beyond, he was convinced that he would never see a more breathtaking, stunning sight in his life.

As he took his first steps into the Nóran capital city of Mór, his opinion did not change.

Still, Mór was a rather striking sight to take in, in its own way.

Buildings carved of grey stone reached toward the sky, almost to the point of looking as though they were stacked atop one another to accommodate more people living inside. The road was paved with cobblestones, horseshoes clacking underfoot in a steady rhythm. On either side of the street walked enormous crowds of people, more than Camaráin had ever seen gathered in one place, almost too many people. He had read in *Broad Generalizations On Which to Base Your Opinions and Personality: The Inquisition's Guide to Dragons (Outdated Edition)* that plagues, wars, and clearance sales at department stores were the three things that would clear the streets in a hurry, and taking four steps inside Mór was enough to make him wish for one of the three.

The tolling of the cathedral bell was enough to send him over the edge. It resounded through the streets, near to quaking them, and almost dropped him to his knees. When he looked down, he was, in fact, on his knees, so if that was the Priory's intent to get people on their knees and pray, well, it was quite effective. He winced, clasping his hands over his ears, while Brían "roared" at the bell, which Camaráin interpreted as the dragon shouting, "Oh yeah, well how do *you* like it?!"

When the bell's echo faded, he unclasped his ears and looked up to Granma, who appeared unfazed by the noise. "Why would anyone live here?" he asked.

Granma crossed her arms. "Look, if you know a better way to buy jewelry, fresh fish, and indulgences from the Priory all at the same store, I'd love to hear it."

"Doesn't the sound bother you, Granma?"

"Oh, I can barely hear anything anymore, dear."

"And the number of people?"

"None of the people here are going to visit Beag—the village is basically a fifty-five-and-over community nowadays."

"Weren't indulgences proven to be fraud so the Priory could get more money?"

Granma pulled a slip of paper out of her pocket and regarded it with suspicion. "Oh, I sure hope not. Where'd you hear that?"

"There was a guy who nailed pieces of wood to the Priory newsletter." Camaráin shrugged. "Ninety-five pieces, I think. Maybe it's still a northern thing. If you put all of them together, maybe you get a prize."

Ma groaned under her breath and rolled her eyes, but Camaráin didn't understand why.

"Anyway," Granma said, hastily shoving the paper back in her pocket and clapping her hands, "shall we be off?"

"Do you know where we're going?" Ma asked.

"Nope." And Granma set forth once more into the breach.

A nervous chill creeped down Camaráin's spine as he clutched to his ma's hand, already feeling the sweat dampening his palm. The pervasive noise of overlapping conversations, horses trotting by, mismatched melodies playing within adjacent pubs, it was all too overwhelming for him to bear. His feet moved him forward, but for all he knew, his body was doing all the work and his mind was just along for the ride.

Taking in the sights of the city was already too much and he closed his eyes, but all that kept him aware of his surroundings were the claws digging into his shoulder. Grimacing, Camaráin looked at Brían, whose attention appeared to be focused else-where, though Camaráin's was more on the clear and present pain burrowing into his skin. "Ow!" he exclaimed. "What are you doing, Brían?"

The dragon did not answer—primarily because he could not yet speak—but he still made inquisitive noises as the family passed an alleyway.

"What's wrong with him?" Ma asked, pulling Camaráin along.

"I have no idea, but he's really—hey!"

Brían leaped off Camaráin's shoulder and scurried across the street, running toward the alley.

"Wait! Brían!" Camaráin released himself from his ma's grip—quite easy, given how slick his hand was—and followed the dragon, leaving behind the concerned and authoritative shouts of his ma and granma. He watched Brían weave his way through the legs of passersby on the opposite sidewalk, much to the varying surprise, annoyance, or otherwise indifference of the citizenry. Camaráin had no choice but to follow, shout-ing "Excuse me!" and "Sorry!" in alternation. This was met with firmer responses from the people of Mór:

"Watch where you're walking, kid!"

"No, you're *in* my *way!"*

"Oh, no, my banana!"

"Why don't you take better care of your rabbit, kid?!"

Drawing a heavy breath once he cleared the throng of peo-ple, Camaráin stared down the length of the alleyway, Brían standing out like a sore thumb. (As a dragon typically would.) He was ready to scold the dragon for being so reckless before his ma and granma arrived to scold him for being so reckless, but a flittering light further down the way caught his eye. Camaráin stopped, narrowing his eyes at the sight. The alleyway reeked, a familiar stench he couldn't place, but that was hardly enough to deter him from remaining where he stood when faced with the light.

Tiny wings beat against the air, keeping aloft a small humanoid form with a face punctuated by dark, beady eyes. Camaráin had seen enough of them in the Crann Woods to mistake this creature for anything else: a faerie. It was fluttering through the alley quite erratically, and he could not say with any certainty if it was because Brían was chasing it. He shuddered, hoping it wouldn't look upon him with those shining, beady eyes, but that didn't matter right now. "Brían!" he hissed. "Get back here!"

The dragon ignored him, following the faerie as it drifted forward, his gait not predatory but rather...playful? He jumped, his wings flapping but doing little to keep him aloft, his front feet swatting at the faerie, who dipped lower and higher as though to goad Brían into trying again. It seemed the dragon had already made another new best friend.

"Oh, come on," Camaráin said, throwing his arms out. "*Again?*"

"Camaráin!" Ma shouted, clearing the crowd with Granma in tow. She appeared quite mad. "What in the world do you think you're—"

"*Shh.*" Camaráin brought a finger to his lips, pointing at the dragon and his new "friend."

The anger was far from leaving her face, but that did not stop the intrigue from flashing in her eyes, if only for a moment.

"Well, how about that," Granma said. "Looks like he's made

another friend."

"I *know*," Camaráin responded through gritted teeth, crossing his arms with a huff. "But why won't he—"

"That's why we're here, isn't it, Cam? If there's anyone who can tell us why he likes the fae more than you, then we—oh, and he's on the move again."

Granma's blunt words aside, Camaráin turned to find Brían chasing the faerie once more, turning the corner until out of sight. "Come on! We need to follow him!"

"Camaráin, you need to stay put, is what you need to do!" Ma shouted.

The boy ignored the order, instead running around the corner. The dank alley opened up to an open square with a small park, a bench placed atop a patch of verdant green grass. Brían jumped on the bench to get a better angle at the faerie, but once again, he missed as the faerie flew out of his reach, sending the dragon face-first into the grass below.

Frustrated and admittedly jealous though he was, Camaráin couldn't prevent the smile stretching across his mouth. Only a small smile, though. He couldn't give the impression he was happy about any of this.

A tug at his collar spun him around. Ma's face was beet-red. "You do *not* run away into a crowd like that, Camaráin, do you understand?"

"Oh, Máirín, he's just a boy chasing his dragon chasing a faerie through a city street," Granma said. "These opportunities don't come often, so seize them."

"Ma, you're not helping."

Regardless, Camaráin looked down at his feet, feeling shame at worrying his ma, and opened his mouth to apologize before his granma spoke once more.

"And off to the races they go again."

Camaráin turned, seeing Brían spinning place as though to locate the faerie. He surveyed the surrounding buildings and alleyways, finding nothing of interest until finally, the glittering light reappeared at the mouth of another alley...though it was a less playful illumination.

Before Camaráin could fully register what happened, a tall man clad in black leathers appeared from the shadows, and in one quick motion, encased the faerie in an iron cage. The man regarded the family in silence while paying no heed to Brían, nodded, and then returned to the shadows.

Brían appeared too stunned to chase, and after a moment, he merely hung his head, grumbling with disappointment and sadness.

The same could be said for the family. "Granma?" Camaráin asked, prying himself free from his ma's clutches. "Do you know who that was?"

With a frown, Granma shook her head. "I can't say for certain but...the costume does look familiar. Where have I seen it before...?" She put a thoughtful hand to her chin but came up with no further words.

Camaráin walked over to the dragon and picked him up, finding no resistance. Brían rested his head atop the boy's shoulders, which was more affection than he had shown in some time.

They spent the rest of the afternoon wandering aimlessly around Mór, but the wind had been taken out of their sails, and the drive to find fae scholars had departed.

Beyond the ice cream, new shoes, fresh colcannon, keychains that read "I ♥ Mór," and a bundle of seven indulgences from the Priory for the price of eight, the family returned to Beag with nothing.

Chapter Nine

"Well, that was interesting."

When Una decided to tail Robeárd's movements today after his voiced intention to "sprinkle a little faerie dust onto tomorrow's breakfast," she couldn't be sure if it was meant literally or if it was code for something else. After watching that family's interaction with the faerie, though, she couldn't be bothered with whatever Robeárd wanted to do with a faerie. At least, not this time.

She had recognized the older woman, having seen her here and there with who she assumed was her husband; and likewise, it was safe to say her accompaniment was her daughter and grandson. As she leaned against the wall, though, allowing the shadows to envelope her, she rested her head against the stone and hummed with interest.

"But, that dragon..." Una murmured, clasping her fingers behind her head. "Never mind how they got a dragon in the first place, but it was *playing* with the faerie..."

Tutting, she eyed the family as they departed the scene, glum faces all. It wasn't lost on Una that they were taken aback by Robeárd's capture of the faerie, but *especially* the dragon.

"Hmm, I wonder...could it be...?"

It had to be, but there was no way she could say for certain. Even though the odds of there actually *being* another hatchling dragon anywhere in Nóra were slim to none, Una was taught gently by her late parents, sternly by the Priory, and quite rudely by the orphanage, that one should not assume. Sure was fun to assume, though.

"I can't say I'm not tempted to follow them." Smacking her lips, she shook her head and walked down the alleyway, curious whether she may be able to pick Robeárd's trail back up. Shouldn't have been hard—the man had never met a trash can he didn't trip over.

But, whoever this family was, it would not be the last she would see of them. Of that, she was certain. "The question is," she muttered, following the trail of upturned trash cans, "where?

"And, how soon?"

Chapter Ten

"**W**ell, the house is still standing, so that's a plus, right?"

Though Camaráin said it in all sincerity and good humor, Granma sighed as though relieved. When one is faced with combustible furniture in the presence of a gnome, a house crumbling to its foundation was not necessarily off the table.

As they approached the door, however, the voices within became clearer, sharper, and no less angry. "At least they had the courtesy to keep the volume down," Granma muttered.

The door swung open, and chairs, tables, and one fern with half of its potting soil strewn about the floor were lined up in the living room, rows alternating between what had been flipped over and what stood in their correct place. Granda and the gnome, just like in the book of the same name, stood facing one another, each huffing and puffing, their breaths sounding like two sheets of sandpaper being rubbed together, as one would do in an everyday circumstance.

"What do you mean, three bundles of wheat for one sheep isn't a fair trade?" Granda rasped. He grabbed the back of the nearest chair and threw it to the ground. "Do you know nothing about supply and demand?"

The gnome responded gnomishly, picked an upturned table

off the ground, and stood it back up.

"You can't say that about the prime minister? We don't *have* a prime minister! What even *is* a prime minister?" Another chair slammed to the ground.

More gnomish nonsense, though to save time, it's best to call it gnonsense. Another table was placed back on its legs.

"Well, it's not my fault they're shaped like that." Down went the chair.

Gnonsense. Up went the table.

They fought over supremacy of the fern, and if the house-plant had a face, well, it didn't anymore.

"Having fun?" Granma asked. Normally, a captive audience would think to clap after a riveting performance, but the ship carrying the theater scene across the channel capsized about twenty years prior, so no one in Nóra had ever seen a riveting performance. No one clapped.

Granda, covered in soil and what remained of that poor fern, tossed the empty planter aside, clonking the gnome in the head, and said, "Oh, hi, dear. Back so soon?"

"It's dusk, Padraig. We've been gone all day."

"Oh. Time flies when you're having..." The concept of "fun" didn't seem to apply here, and neither Granda nor the gnome appeared to have the wherewithal to assert to the contrary. The gnome merely sneered at Granda, to which the man said, "Quiet, you."

"What are you two arguing about, Da?" Ma asked.

"Oh, not a clue. I haven't the faintest idea of what he's saying."

"Why were you arguing to begin with, then?"

Granda shrugged. "Why do any of us argue, in the grand

scheme of things?"

"Oh, Lord, he's delirious now," Granma said. "Camaráin, get him some water and a leek stalk from the kitchen, would you?"

Camaráin took two steps toward the kitchen, slipping on a pile of dirt in the process, before asking, "What's the leek for?"

"So I can hit him for making this mess."

"What about for the gnome?"

"Grab a leek for all of us, and maybe he'll finally leave."

"Hey, hey, wait!" Granda said, holding his palms out. "There's no need to kick him out yet."

Granma blinked with disbelief. "He blew up our couch—"

"It got better."

"—and then you argued with him for eight hours straight."

"Four hours. We took a nap for a bit."

"I don't know what's happening anymore."

Ma flashed a glance at Camaráin. "Have we lost sense of the plot or something?"

The boy shrugged and looked at Brían. "Do you have any-thing to add?"

The dragon jumped off Camaráin's shoulders and wove his way through the upturned furniture and piles of dirt, finding his way to the couch and the book on tall ships that lay open.

"Well, I guess that answers that."

"Anyway," Granda began, "I don't remember why we were fighting to begin with." He turned to the gnome. "Can I interest you in the pub?"

For once, the gnome did not respond with belligerence. He puffed out his bottom lip and shrugged as if to say, "My only other plan this evening was to be a general pain in your rear end but if I get a free drink out of it, then count me in." Few friendships were started for less.

As Granda and the gnome made for the door, Ma raised a hand. "Um, Da? Isn't the Priory hunting fae creatures right now? Do you think it's a good idea to bring him with you?"

"Good point." Granda flicked the gnome's hat off his head and replaced it with one of his own, a bucket hat that read "Kiss Me, I'm Pretending to Be Nóran for a Laugh." One had to squint to read all the text, especially toward the end when they ran out of space. "There. Now I can say he's my cousin."

"You don't have a cousin, Padraig," Granma said.

"I do now. Come along, cousin!"

Cousin Gnome was happy to oblige, and the two walked into the dusk, the pub calling their names.

Everyone else looked at one another in stunned silence. They all tiptoed around the mess, preferring to ignore its existence, and went about their evenings. Camaráin grabbed a book off the shelf called *This is <u>Really</u> Dragon Along* and sat beside Brían.

When he opened the book, the pages were blank, which just made a strange day even stranger.

Days passed, Camaráin still lacked the Bond between himself and Brían, and the talk of the village was the arrival of Granda's long-lost cousin who had forgotten the Nóran tongue due to an unfortunate run-in with a boar, seven potatoes, a diving helmet, and a poorly-assembled pillow. The crowds took to inventing witchcraft, and then blaming it.

Peace was well enough restored to Granma and Granda's

house, which otherwise remained in tatters while Granma re-fused to clean the mess that had been left, whilst Granda spent his days at the pub in the name of maintaining peace with the gnome. Sacrifices were made by all.

Over the past few days, Camaráin took the opportunity to survey any book his grandparents had available for anything at all on dragons, the fae, and the connection between them, but answers could not be found in Granda's *Pictures of Warships for Dads to Talk About* series or Granma's recipe books and romance novels. Camaráin did see a book titled *50 Scales of Gray*, but Granma quickly took it away from him before he could get past page one, informing him it was "not that kind of book."

Needless to say, he was growing frustrated, and Brían's indif-ference toward the matter, as well as the interest the dragon placed on the book with pictures of bridge structures from the mainland, only exacerbated it.

But on this day, a knock at the door spelled an end to the frustration. Or, at the least, an end to hunger, judging from the aroma.

Ma opened the door and smiled. "Hi, Áine. Thanks for com-ing."

"I'm not tipping you for dragging the carriage yourself. It's not my fault your horse got stolen!" Áine stuck her tongue out at whomever she was talking to outside, and rushed to close the door behind her before she could be prodded further. The handle of a wicker basket was looped around her arm, its contents covered by a gingham hand towel.

"Fun ride, I take it?" Ma placed a hand on Áine's shoulder and guided her around the piles of dirt on the floor.

"I honestly think I prefer when the Inquisition was just bad at being the Inquisition instead of being bad at everything else. Why is there dirt everywhere?"

Ma opted not to answer the question, and instead brought her to a clean corner of the house. "Thank you for coming down."

The expression on Áine's face did not indicate happiness. "When I said, 'reach out to me if you need anything,' I didn't quite mean *'anything.'* But..." She waved at Camaráin, then looked past him and at Brían, who had still not looked up from his book. "So, you think he's part-gnome?"

"Yes," Camaráin said.

"No," Ma said more forcefully.

Áine knew just who to trust more on the matter. She looked even less happy now. With a defeated sigh, she unwrapped the basket and reached inside. "I brought a couple pies." All the tables remained upturned. "So...where do I...?"

Ma guided her once more through the obstacle course and to the kitchen. Granma had been sitting in there as one of the few places that had not faced the wrath of Granda and the gnome, and so pleasant introductions were exchanged, replete with all the confusion and one would expect of the...everything that had transpired in the living room. Camaráin followed, his stomach growling at the smell of the pie, and picked Brían up, his claw still holding tight to the book.

When he entered the kitchen, Áine was already cutting the pie into slices, and he was sneaking under her arm to snatch a slice.

"Camaráin!" Ma shouted.

"Brían's hungry!"

The dragon shook his head, his attention remaining on the book.

Áine eyed the dragon with interest. "Definitely not like Pilib, is he?"

"That's putting it lightly," Camaráin muttered, pouting. "He likes the gnome more than he likes me."

"Right…" She looked at Ma. "Your letter asked what I knew of gnomes. Maybe it's time I got the full story?"

With pie distributed, they returned to the living room, all squeezing in on the couch to maintain Granma's cold war with Granda about cleaning the house. Ma and Camaráin took turns detailing the events of the last few days, from Brían's instant rapport with Cousin Gnome to the chase in Mór for the faerie and its resultant capture by that mysterious man in black. Granma then spent a long time talking about the mess caused by the arguments that left the house in such a state. It was an awkward rant for all.

When at last there was long enough of a silence to ask, Ma jumped in to say, "Long story short, Áine, how much do you know of gnomes?"

Shrugging, Áine said, "Very little, honestly. Adhamh was the only one with whom I interacted with any regularity, so I'm not sure whether to thank or curse Iósaf for that." Granma's eyes widened at the mention of Iósaf, and she opened her mouth to inquire further, but Áine continued before allowing the opportunity. "I'm sure you can tell that gnomes aren't a personable sort, save for when they're forced to collect desserts on behalf of someone else."

Granma's excitement disappeared.

"But what about their relationship with dragons?" Camaráin

asked. "Adhamh didn't care about Pilib, and Pilib didn't immediately become best friends with Adhamh. But Brían is the opposite: he can't be bothered with us but only wants to be friends with the gnome."

Áine leaned back and rested a hand on her chin. "Interesting..."

"And same with that faerie in Mór! He ran after it without a second thought and he made Ma really mad at me when I chased him."

"*He's* not the one who made me mad," Ma muttered under her breath.

Ignoring Ma's remark like an obedient son, Camaráin added, "There has to be *something* you've read about it. Anything at all."

The former Draconic Priest remained deep in thought, closing her eyes. "I remember a story where a dragon bred with a donkey, but..." She trailed off, her voice barely audible.

Camaráin raised an eyebrow. "What does that have to do with anything?"

"Huh? Oh, sorry, I was still on that part-gnome thing. It wouldn't happen, maybe." Áine glanced at Brían, the dragon paying her little mind. "I'm not entirely sure, if I'm honest. But I would welcome a visit to the libraries in Mór to find out."

Chapter Eleven

Áine took to the streets of Mór with far greater enthusiasm than Camaráin would have expected for someone who had spent so much time living in the woods. Not that there was a correlation between the two, it was a safe assumption that living in solitude within a dense forest did not quite translate to, "I can't wait for it to take three times as long to get where I'm going because this family of tourists thinks it's necessary to take up the entire sidewalk and point at every building, street sign, and shadow they see."

If Áine couldn't have been fussed with that, she didn't look it. A wide smile stretched across her face, more exuberant than at any other point Camaráin had seen her. She craned her head back, drawing in a deep breath, humming with satisfaction, drawing perplexed looks from Camaráin as well as his ma and granma. "Ah, smell that air!"

The air smelled of smokestacks and body odor. "No, thank you," Camaráin said.

Flashing a smirk, Áine turned on her heel and pushed through a family that was in the way. Some locals caught sight of that and followed suit. Ever the trendsetter, that one.

"Áine, wait!" Ma called out, barreling past the shoved-aside tourist family as a means to fit in with the cool crowd. The tourists, for their part, pointed at one another, unsure of where to divert their attention whilst being spun around. "Áine! Do you know where you're going?"

At the head of the crowd, Áine raised a hand, and her flock parted in an impressive display of power (or a display of kindness from considerate locals, but that doesn't make for as riveting of storytelling). "It's not the first time I've been here, Máirín. It's been a long time, though. I hadn't a clue when I'd next be able to come back."

"Did you grow up here, Áine?" Granma asked, now standing amongst the rest of the family at the head of the crowd.

Áine shook her head. "Oh, no. My childhood was spent up north with the rest of the Draconic Priests. My studies would just take me here from time to time. It's much more exciting here than reading by candlelight in a dank, dripping cave or some field where there's not another living soul for miles."

Camaráin shrugged, Brían following suit. "That doesn't sound too bad. Plenty of time to read."

"I know it's overwhelming, Cam," she said, placing a comforting hand on his free shoulder. "But it's not so scary once you get used to it. I mean, look at all these nice people." She held her hand out to her gathered flock, the front rows smiling and waving.

"Hey lady, why don't you shut your mouth and get moving?!" shouted a tourist at the back.

Áine jumped off the sidewalk and into the street. "Why don't you go point at rocks, ya twit?!"

"We already did." The voice was lower and much meeker. And that was that.

"Anyway," Áine continued, the pep returned to her step, "shall we be off to the library? I can't wait to see what they've added to their collections." She reached for Camaráin's arm to pull him along but missed and grabbed Brían's front leg instead. The dragon dangled behind her, apathy clear upon his face. At this point, it was probably the closest he could get to flying.

Camaráin scampered after her, Ma and Granma following at their own pace. When they were last in Mór several days ago, he did not give himself the opportunity to take in the sights and sounds of the city, being too distracted first by Brían chasing after the faerie, and next by growing too upset at the faerie's sudden capture to focus on much else.

But as he chased after Áine, a gentle sea breeze blowing his hair back, the grey stone buildings towering above him in a feat of engineering and construction, the city square rich in character with its central fountain spurting water from a lion's head (which made little sense for numerous reasons, chief among them being no one in Nóra had ever seen a lion and likely had no idea what a lion was, so how this fountainhead came to be was a mystery, as was its architect), the people hawking fresh goods in the central market like mutton and fish and clothes that their unfaithful spouses no longer needed, he took all of it in for the first time, and came to realize that he still did not particularly care for any of it. Also, his shoe was untied but he was too afraid to kneel in the crowd to retie it.

For all the overwhelming stress of having to following Áine at such a pace to not lose sight of her, it was worth it when he laid eyes on the library. It was the largest building he had ever seen. He was familiar with Lord Saibhir's mansion on the outskirts of Baile, mainly because the village newsletter for several months consisted only of a picture of the dwelling with the words, "Hey, look at this, peasants!" scribbled on top. He didn't think anything existed in Nóra with the same grandeur, but *this* was impressive. All the tall buildings of Mór were carved in the same flat stone facing, because all the designers with actual talent were employed at the library.

Tall granite columns lined the walkway, which led to a set of stairs leading up to the library proper. The façade of the library had mythological creatures carved into it, from unicorns to griffons to a middle-aged Nóran man who still had all his hair. Above the façade were the letters "L I B R I" engraved into the stone, and Camaráin wondered why they got so lazy that they couldn't finish spelling "library." Surrounding the entryway was an assortment of shrubberies, ferns, and other greenery he had no particular interest in. He was raring to go inside, to the point he didn't realize he was already trying to walk in, heedless of his ma holding him by his collar. A smooth path had been worked underfoot.

"Going somewhere?" Ma asked, a soft smirk on her face.

"I would be, if you'd let me go," Camaráin said.

"Now, now, Cam," Granma said. "You can't go running off like that."

"Sure I can." Despite his insistence, he was presently unable to go running off like that.

"You wouldn't even know where to begin," Áine said, amusement in her eyes. "And I'm sure you'd only faint from getting yourself all riled up."

"I wouldn't! Maybe. That only happened once."

Chuckling, Áine looked at her hand to see Brían hanging slack in her grip, mostly just happy to be there. She righted the dragon onto his feet and ran a hand down his neck. "Do you want to go through some books, Brían?"

The dragon was already running before she finished the question. No longer any point in waiting around, then.

Camaráin took off after the dragon, the adults close behind, and by the time they caught up with Brían, the hatchling was scratching at the door, furiously searching for a way inside. Picking the dragon off the ground, Camaráin placed him on his shoulder, per usual, and entered. And very nearly fainted. Áine knew what she was talking about. She was also there to catch him before his left his feet.

When his vision returned, he was brought near to fainting again. Curse those overwhelming sights.

Third time was the charm: it was even more stunning than he could have dreamed. Books stretched as far as the eye could see, rows upon rows of tomes ancient and newborn, the scent of fresh pages filling the air. In the corner, a family of tourists were pointing at a closed window. The bookshelves were beautifully crafted, works of art unto themselves with stories unto themselves carved into their frames. It was as near to heaven as he could ever imagine.

"Well, then," Áine said, planting an excited hand on his shoulder. "Are you ready to learn?"

"Yeah?" Worded like that, it almost sounded like school-work. Camaráin was torn as to how much enthusiasm he should show for such a thing.

Ma sighed behind him. "You ready to read about dragons or something?" she deadpanned.

"Let's go!" Much more excitement this time.

"Play to your audience, Áine," Ma said with a wink.

Before they could progress further, a library attendant walked up to Camaráin. "Excuse me, young man. I'm sorry, but we do not allow pets in the library. You'll have to leave your dog outside."

Camaráin looked at Brían, who seemed offended at being called a dog. If only he knew how great dogs were. "Oh, Brían isn't my dog. He's my—" He almost said "dragon," but that probably would have complicated matters, so instead, he said, "cousin?"

"Oh," the attendant said. He passed a second glance at Brían and said, "Your cousin's ugly." And he walked away.

Brían looked even more offended.

"How rude," Granma said.

"Don't get upset, Brían," Camaráin said, comforting the dragon. "You take after me."

The dragon craned his head, staring at Camaráin.

"He might not know whether to take that as a compliment," Ma japed. She pushed the boy along. "Alright, Áine? You lead the way."

With a nod and a flourish, the former Draconic Priest did as requested, leading the pack through the whisper-quiet corridors of the library. It was a welcomed reprieve from the hustle and bustle of the Nóran streets, such that, besides the tourists pointing at specks of dirt and the library attendant who thought Brían was ugly, Camaráin saw hardly another soul within the library's depths. Here and there, someone moved out of the corner of his eye, but other than that, no one made a noise. That could have been by design, but Camaráin had never been inside a library, so who was he to judge?

Áine hummed with delight as she wove through the tight

confines, passing by sections with labels such as *Mathematics, Cooking, Literary Fiction, Illiterary Fiction*, and *Miscellaneous & Et Cetera*. There were too many titles for Camaráin to take in, though there were a few which caught his eye in the variety section titled *The Prophet of Profit: Eventually the Scratch Ticket Will Work* and *The Great Inquisition War Map: Coloring Book Edition (Green Crayon Now Included)*. He mentally jotted both down for later.

Eventually, Áine stopped in front of a section labeled *Cultural Resources*. "This may be what we're looking for," she said, shuffling inside.

Camaráin followed, his breath catching at the impressive array of tomes. A quick glance at the shelf labels indicated much of the books had to do with Nóran folklore, history, and mythology. There was a multi-volume set on the Ulcer Cycle (and the exploits and adventures of its hero Hoo Hooligan), a handwritten recollection of the Biking Raids of three centuries past (the end of which resulted in bicycles forever being banned from Nóra), and a large tome titled *An Oral History of the Succession Wars*. He took it off the shelf and opened it, revealing only a single page that read, "Please revisit in a few centuries when audiobooks have been invented." Not knowing what that meant, Camaráin carefully placed it back where it was.

"Cam, look!" Ma said, pointing further down the aisle. "They've added a dragon section!"

His eyes lighting up, Camaráin rushed forward. "They have dragon books?"

Áine looked at the shelf. "Well, they've added a dragon *book*." She pointed at a hastily scribbled piece of tape placed along the ridge of the shelf that indeed said only, "**DRAGON BOOK**."

Camaráin peered at the shelf, and saw it carried only *Up-scaled: The Official Novelization of the Novel*. "Hmph, boring. I already know what happens in that one." His gaze drifted down, noting something of interest. Kneeling to the bottom shelf, he said, "Huh, there's nothing down here. But...Áine, look at this." He pointed to the collection of dust—or rather, the lines of dust indicating books were here recently.

"Yeah, I noticed that," Áine said. "Take a look right here, too." She pointed at a painted-over section of the shelf where something was once etched, though it was poorly done and still clearly read *Fae*.

"Huh," Ma said. Turning to Granma, she said, "Do you think it's to do with those fae hunts you mentioned, Ma?"

Granma furrowed her brow, stroking her chin thoughtfully. "But why would they take the books off the shelves? And where would they go?"

"Maybe they're all behind this curtain?" Áine pointed at a black curtain at the end of the aisle with the word ***BANNED*** swathed across it in red paint.

Ma chuckled. "Come on, Áine. It wouldn't be that easy."

Áine pulled the curtain, revealing shelves upon shelves of books on the fae. "No one would be *that* dumb, Máirín."

As she walked beyond the curtain, a passerby remarked, "Woah, there's more behind there?" and then kept walking.

Her shoulders slumped, but she let it pass. "Camaráin, you and Brían come with me. Máirín and Aindréa, if you two wouldn't mind keeping watch?"

Everyone nodded and set to their respective tasks.

For his part, Camaráin followed Áine behind the curtain, with just enough light filtering through for the books to be legible. His attention was drawn to books like *I Am Faerie and Faerie Is Me: A Journey of Self-Discovery and Self-Forgettery* and *Granda and the Gnome 2: This Time It's Personal*, but there were so many books that he hardly knew where to begin. "What should I look for, Áine?" he asked, turning to the Draconic Priest.

Áine did not answer, her hand reaching for a book whose title Camaráin could not read.

"Áine? What is it?"

She hummed to herself as she flipped through the book.

"Áine? Hello?" He tugged at the hem of her shirt.

She startled, nearly dropping the book. "What is it?" she hissed. There was a fire in her eyes as she stared him down.

Camaráin took a step back, his heart skipping a beat while Brían spread his wings wide in a show of strength. "Sorry, Áine. I just wanted to know what I should be looking for."

The blaze quelled, and she calmed. "No, *my* apologies, Cam. I didn't mean to frighten you." She gestured to the book in her hand. "Though, I think I'm on the right track here."

Narrowing his eyes, Camaráin read the title as *Politics, Discourse, and the Verbal Tomfoolery of the Land of Fae*. It seemed a bit above his understanding. "What is it?"

Áine smiled. "Inter-fae relations, and extra-fae relations. If there's anything to do with fae interaction with dragons, this may be the place to start. And, if I remember correctly..." She flipped to the index at the rear of the book, and then redirected to her destination. "Here we are. Selkies."

Camaráin inclined his head. He had heard of selkies only

insofar that a book at home had the word *selkies* in the title, but who or what they were, that was beyond him.

Skimming through the pages, Áine said, "I can't say I've ever encountered a selkie. They're water dwellers, so no reason for me to come across one in the Crann Woods. A bit tricksy and duplicitous, though. I wonder..." She looked at Brían, her eyes lingering on the dragon for a long while.

Brían seemed to take her up on the staring contest, not breaking his sight from her.

Raising an eyebrow, Camaráin asked, "What? What do you wonder?"

Before Áine could answer, though, Ma's voice hissed on the other end of the curtain. "We're not alone out here!"

Footsteps grew louder, drawing nearer. Before Camaráin had a chance to register what was happening, the curtain flew open, revealing a young woman with dark hair and piercing eyes staring down at him. Beyond her, Ma and Granma stood and watched helplessly, shrugging as if to say, "Welp, what can you do?"

The young woman smiled. "Well, she's right," she said. "You weren't alone out here."

Chapter Twelve

"**M**áirín! Aindréa!" Áine hissed. "I told you to keep watch!"

"We did keep watch," Ma said, shrugging again. "We watched her walk right past us and through the curtain."

"How helpful."

Camaráin backed away as far as he could, clutching a growling Brían in his arms. He reached behind, furiously searching for the wall, the new arrival staring at him all the while. Though he had often read of secret passageways tucked in the walls and crevices of great libraries, he was disappointed to learn that the wall behind him was nothing but brick and maybe some lettuce from someone's salad. A door labeled "Break Room" was beside him, though no one within seemed to make note of or care for their presence in the restricted area.

"It's not our fault," Granma asserted, planting her hands on her hips. "For all we know, she could have been perched on top of the bookshelves like a cat."

The look in the young woman's eyes indicated she did not disagree. It only made Camaráin more suspicious of her. That, and the fact she was just silently staring at him and Áine for quite some time. She seemed to be ignoring Brían, though. The dragon continued to growl, regardless.

Áine smacked her lips and threw her arms out at her side, the silence lingering for too long. "So, what happens now? Do I talk first? Do you? The boy? The dragon? What do you want?"

"Áine!" Camaráin said, eyes widening. "Why are you calling my cousin a dragon?"

"Why are you calling a dragon your cousin?" the woman asked blithely. She appeared more confused than intrigued.

Camaráin sputtered at the bluntness of her words. "Oh...um. He had an unfortunate accident with...um...witches crafting?"

"'Witchcraft,' Cam," Áine whispered.

"No one would fall for that. You realize that, right?" the woman said.

"You'd be surprised."

Applying gentle pressure to the dragon's head to get him to stop growling, Camaráin took a deep breath, maintaining his distance from the woman. Meanwhile, Brían continued to growl.

"Now, then," Áine said, holding an outstretched arm in front of Camaráin. "I'll ask again: what do you want? Who are you?"

The young woman straightened, brushing dust off the sleeves of her shirt. "Oh, how rude of me. My name is Una." She looked around the enclosure, tutting her lips. "Brave of you to boldly travel beyond the bedsheet of forbidden knowledge. I don't know that anyone's tried that."

"Your sarcasm is hilarious."

"Sarcasm?" Una raised an eyebrow. "In Mór? No, not at all."

Áine grunted with bemusement.

"No, I'm serious. We don't use sarcasm in Mór. No one's actually gone beyond this curtain."

"Real stickler for the rules here, then."

Una shook her head. "No, it's just that's the only door to the break room." She pointed at the door beside Camaráin. Someone within was staring into a sandwich with his fingers gripping what remained of his hair. He seemed on his last nerve, or the sandwich was really bad.

"Rather inconvenient."

"You're telling me. Did you know that's the only break room in the library, too? And they only get a fifteen-minute break, half of that spent walking here. I'd argue that's more than a little inconvenient, wouldn't you?"

Áine blinked at her. "I really don't care. I'm just going to get back to reading this if you're only here to waste our time."

Una smirked. "Sampling the forbidden knowledge then, are we?"

"It can't be *that* forbidden. Clearly the books were just recently moved." Áine pointed to the dust marks on the bottom shelf outside of the curtain. "Besides, you can read these books literally anywhere else."

"Hmph, I shouldn't have to leave my hometown just to read a book." Una pouted, crossing her arms.

"Not my problem. Now, if you'll excuse me, I'd like to—"

The break room door flew open before Áine could finish, the man with the disappointing sandwich gripping the doorknob so tightly it looked near enough to snapping off. "Will you be *quiet*! I only have twenty-eight seconds left to eat!" His face was beet-red. So was his sandwich, its contents dripping on the table. Maybe it was blood. Camaráin wasn't one to judge.

"Seems you're wasting those seconds," Áine said, grinning.

"Gah!" the man shouted. "Now it's twenty-one seconds!"

"Shh!" Camaráin put a finger to his lips. "We're in a library, sir."

"What's your point?"

Camaráin was taken aback. "Oh, um. Aren't you supposed to be quiet in the library? I read that in a book once and—"

"A *book*?! Where do you think we are, a library? Gah! Three seconds!" He ran back to the table, but before he made it back, two broad-shouldered men appeared from the shadows and threw the remains of his sandwich out the window, and then started lightly kicking him in the shins for good measure.

Suddenly, the old Nóran adage, "He who pays heed not to the clock shall be he who pays in shins not unbruised" made far more sense to Camaráin.

The man, his shins thoroughly bruised, was carried off and pushed through a hidden door in the break room wall. Unfair that the hidden rooms were in places Camaráin had no access to.

As the pained whimpers faded, and the thought of how much food was just wasted passed between each of them, Una broke the silence to say, "Well, I didn't come here to bother you just for kicks."

Áine had returned her attention to the book in hand but sighed with annoyance and looked back up at Una. "Then, please. Do tell. I'm ever so eager to know why you're bothering us."

Camaráin, for his part, felt his face blanch. "Are we in trouble?" he asked.

A smile spread across Una's face, one that felt far less intimidating than the one she had entered the banned section with. "Oh, no. Not at all, little one. I must admit, I've been looking for you for a few days now."

Ma stepped forward. "Excuse me?" Her nostrils flared. "What do you want from us?"

Una turned, her smile remaining. "Oh, it's less what *I* want. I think it's better to say what *we* want. After all..." She redirected her eyes to Brían, and the dragon quieted, strangely. An inquisitive glint shone in the hatchling's eyes. "You may be just who I'm looking for, but more importantly, *I* may be just who *you're* looking for."

Chapter Thirteen

Traipsing around the alleyways of Mór was less exciting when not chasing a dragon chasing a faerie, but such was the hand they were dealt.

If anything, it felt more harrowing. Despite how empty the library was, Camaráin couldn't help but feel that Una was secreting them away to somewhere they weren't supposed to be. Granted, she *was*, though after the last adventure, Camaráin was accustomed to sneaking about, learning about creatures those more powerful than him said were "evil" or "banned" or "rather spooky and creepy."

Yes, the last one was just his own thoughts, but he had to assume someone among the Priory higher-ups was wary of the fae. They had to have *some* reason to hunt them and pretend they didn't exist, after all.

All the same, even as he had the protection of Áine and Granma in front of him and Ma behind, and despite there no longer being a need to worry of it, he hid Brían in his bag, much to the dragon's displeasure. The hatchling scurried about within, likely first to find a comfortable spot, then to be inconvenient. A part of Camaráin wished Brían was more like Pilib, if only in this instance.

The alleyways Una led them down made for tight and narrow quarters, more so than those they had explored some days earlier. Camaráin could already feel himself growing disoriented. Looking up, all he could see was the same cloudy sky and the same grey rain-stained buildings. Everything looked alike, and for all he knew, Una was leading them in circles. At one point, she did, just for a laugh, but that was the only time it didn't feel like it.

After minutes or hours or days—who could really be sure?—Una stopped in front of them, hands on her hips, nodding to herself.

"We're here?" Áine asked, holding her hand out to Camaráin so he didn't walk into her.

"Huh?" Una said. She blinked, holding up a finger, and then ushered them further along with a wave of her hand. "Sorry. Was just keeping an ear open."

"Why?" Granma said. "What's there to be—"

"Plenty, so long as I'm able to hear it. Now, please, if you would?"

"Sorry."

"Sorry."

"Uh?"

And an ever ferocious "roar" from within the bag to round it all out.

"Oh, Lord have mercy," Una muttered, quickening her pace.

It was difficult to tell whether she was moving quicker to abandon this errand, or if there was actually something worth their worry, but they kept in step with Una just the same, puddles splashing underfoot in a steady rhythm.

Una stopped for a second time, holding up her palm once

more. The ghost of a smile stretched across her lips. "Now we're here."

The alleyway had opened up, no longer constrained to such tight quarters, and shops lined either side of the narrow walkway. Candlelit windows invited passersby in, though from how quiet things were, Camaráin wondered how much business these places drew, and what type of people, for that matter.

His attention, however, was drawn to the shop Una had stopped in front of. He looked at the façade, which read *Sea Louse Tea House*.

"Not quite an inviting name," Ma muttered.

Una shrugged. "Exactly what we would want, no?"

"Aren't you worried about someone only reading the words 'Tea House' and walking in?"

"This is Mór. Anyone has a thirst, they go to a pub instead."

"Why?" Camaráin asked.

Ma tussled the top of his head. "You'll understand when you have kids."

For a back-alley tea shop, it smelled quite nice inside. A lovely aroma of lavender and lilac wafted through the air, and the faint smell of chamomile and green teas tickled at Camaráin's nostrils. Green tea was a relatively new development in Nóra. It had been brought over from the far east by explorers from the mainland, who would later claim to have invented such a tea because someone on the ship dropped a potted plant into some drinking water and couldn't be bothered to take it out. The novelty of such innovation was enough to bring folks out in droves to try this new beverage.

Despite the pleasant smells, though, the shop was empty, the only noise coming from the pub a few shops down, which was quite raucous for it not even being noon yet. Small wooden tables were lined up in rows, still shining in the daylight as though they were just cleaned. On the wall hung sketches that may as well have been to maintain appearances, because they were terrible. In the corner stood a metal bookcase filled with books with unmarked spines, and one book with the title *Hidden Door Switch* scribbled on it. Camaráin's confusion was not lost on Una, who grinned and gestured toward the bookcase.

Camaráin narrowed his gaze and watched her, his curiosity piqued as the marked book caught in a hitch as Una pulled it. The bookcase swung forward, bringing with it a section of the wall. "Oh, that's not good!" he said, pointing at the damage. "What are we gonna do? The wall is broken!"

Ma leaned in close. "None of your books had hidden doors in them, did they?"

"Oh."

Una strained with the effort of pulling the hidden door open, while also wincing at the scrape of metal on the ground. "He's not too far from the truth. This hidden door came with the shop. We only found out when someone fell through the wall."

"How does one 'fall through' a stone wall?" Granma asked.

"The guy had a hard head," Una said with a shrug.

"What do you mean, 'the hidden door came with the shop?'"

"Exactly as I say. Used to be Mór was a dry city. Folk weren't too happy about that. Took to operating pubs and distilleries and aquariums in their cellars. Now folk can let loose on Sundays in accordance with the Priory's teachings."

"Only on Sundays?" Áine asked. "How do the pubs stay open the rest of the week? Why else would people go to them?"

"The ambiance, mostly."

"This city is weirder than I remember," Áine said to Ma, her voice kept to a hush.

Una gestured them through the opening, ensuring to close it after they had all entered. The screeching from the scraping metal brought a twitch to Camaráin's eye, and a roar from his bag. The canvas was near to ripping from the strength of Brían's claws.

A set of stone stairs spiraled further underground, the steps illuminated by lit sconces adorning the walls. The flames danced as Una led them down, a hushed commotion growing louder the further they descended. They came to a closed door, light wafting out from underneath.

When Una opened it, the commotion stopped, a collective breath drawn in, and a small group of people with books opened before them stared at the new arrivals. Camaráin could not help but notice shock in the eyes of a few of them.

"Una?" a stocky man asked, small spectacles balanced on the bridge of his nose. He crossed his arms, a shadow cast over his eyes as he furrowed his brow. "Who are these people?"

Another man stood, rushing past Camaráin and company to shut the door, latching a lock in the process. "We have told you time and again that you are not to bring—"

"Oh, calm yourselves," Una said, waving a hand. "I promise this isn't like the last time."

"You mean, when you brought an *Inquisitor* down here?"

"I didn't know it at the time. Besides, what can the Inquisition do about the fae? They can barely do anything about dragons."

Camaráin's eyes lit up, and he stepped forward, pushing past Una. "The fae? You mean you're..." He trailed off, his breath catching as he took in the sight. Bookshelves lined the walls, these with marked spines and mostly sporting titles with reference to the fae. His first instinct was to rush toward the nearest shelf and grab the first book he could find. His second instinct was to stay put as Ma's fingers dug into his shoulder, preventing him from moving forward. He opted to listen to Ma this time.

"Una, I ask again," said the first man, closing the book in front of him and pushing his spectacles further up his nose. "Who *are* these people?"

"I found them at the library," Una responded, her voice deadpan.

"...And?"

"In the *banned* section."

The man rolled his eyes. "Isn't that how you found that Inquisitor?"

"Yes, but this is for a different reason."

"Oh? And what's that?"

Brían scurried within Camaráin's bag, nearly knocking the boy off his feet until finally he leaped out, nearly tearing a hole in the bag, his ruby-red wings flapping, slowing his descent as he glided to the ground. He drew heaving breaths over the floor, his eyes wide, and Camaráin bared his teeth in embarrassment at the realization the dragon was probably short on breath.

Una pointed at the hatchling, ignoring his wheezes as he drew in breath, and said, "*That* would be why."

"Why'd you bring a cat in here?" the stocky man asked.

"It's a dragon, you stooge."

The man scoffed. "Do I look like some sort of Draconic

Priest or something?"

"No, I wouldn't say you look like me," Áine said. "More to the point—what's going on here? Who are you? Why are we here? And how long ago was prohibition? It *still* smells like stout and mint julep in here."

Una held up a finger and—raising additional fingers in turn—said, "In order: this is a place where we can research the fae in peace. We are fae researchers—don't worry too much about them, they're not plot-relevant. You're here because I had you follow me. And prohibition ended several years back. We kept the bar but forgot to put windows in."

"Fae researchers?" Camaráin repeated. He turned and flashed a grin at Ma and Granma. "Granda was right! We *did* find them!"

"You were right to seek us out, Camaráin," Una said, kneeling beside him, smiling first at him, and then at Brían, who continued to hack again the floor. "Your dragon indeed has a connection to the fae."

"Huh?" Pursing his lips, Camaráin looked at Granma. "Shouldn't we be worrying about getting the gnome out of Granma and Granda's house, though?"

Áine pushed him aside. "More important things right now, Cam." Granma furrowed her brow at Áine, but the Draconic Priest paid her no mind. "We *were* also trying to discover Brían's connection to the fae, remember?"

"Oh yeah."

"You were on the right track in the library, Áine," Una confirmed. "There is a selkie in these lands...a selkie who may well be happy to see the dragon."

Brían looked up at Una, exhaustion on his face, but breathing normally once more. He flashed a sneer at Camaráin's bag and looked as though he wanted to light it ablaze.

The smile on Una's face, however, began to fade. "There's...one small issue, though."

"Yeah?" Áine asked. "And what's that?"

"The Priory is also hunting her."

"Yeah, that's par for the course, isn't it?"

Chapter Fourteen

"What do you mean, they're hunting her?" Camaráin asked, reaching down to clutch Brían tight, against the dragon's best wishes. "Is there another Inquisition we don't know about now?"

Una smacked her lips together and surveyed the room, slowly panning her head over the scene. "Not as such. But perhaps just as annoying."

"It has to do with the bans on fae scholarship, doesn't it?" Ma asked. She turned to Granma and added, "You mentioned something about the Priory hunting fae, didn't you?"

Granma nodded. "And we saw that faerie captured by that man in black the other day, as well." She looked at Una. "So, you mean to say..."

With a slow nod and a frown stretching across her lips, Una said, "Precisely so."

Camaráin's eyes widened. "That man is gonna put *you* in a cage next?"

"No, Cam," Ma assured. "That's very illegal." Hesitation gripped her, and she turned back to Una to ask, "...Right?"

"Oh, yes, very much so." Una affirmed. "The Common Human Rights and General Decency Act from a couple years back made sure of that."

"What is wrong with this city?" Áine muttered.

"Anyway," Una continued, ignoring Áine, "I mean to say, Aindréa, that the Priory has employed a group of hunters for just that purpose. To capture fae."

"An Inquisition that's *actually* under the Priory's purview," Áine said.

"You could consider them to be more of a mercenary sort, or independent contractors. Either way, they've made their presence well-known here in Mór in recent years."

There had been a few stories that Camaráin read which featured mercenaries—namely, the dark and aptly-named *Captain Hannibal and the Sunshine Quartet* early reader series—but he never thought they actually existed. He always thought them something that existed only to serve a narrative purpose rather than an actual one, like hard-boiled detectives or corned beef and cabbage, but that these hunters were not only real, but in the employ of the holiest seat in Nóra, stretched the limits of his belief, which was already growing thin these days.

"I take it you've run afoul with them, then?" Áine asked. She gnawed at her lower lip, her years of solitude in the Crann Woods clearly still weighing on her.

"To some degree, yes," Una said, "though I'd wager not to the extent the Inquisition hassled you."

"'Hassled' is certainly one way to put it. A horrible way, but still *a* way."

Her hands clasped behind her back, Una circled the group, letting Áine's comment pass once more. She glanced at the bookshelves and all the contents within, and sighed. "There aren't laws in place that prohibit us from reading and researching the fae. It's more of a 'being able to read in peace and quiet' thing than anything else. Try going to any open space topside with a book referencing the fae, and you'll inevitably get questions like, 'Why are you reading that?' and 'The Priory is gonna get proper mad with you,' and 'I voted against the General Decency Act,' even though we don't put things to vote here. We, ourselves, are safe from all but annoyance.

"The fae, though," she continued, "it's a tougher go for them. Why the Priory decided to ban and hunt them in the capital region, it's not for me to say. Folks with power just like to...*do* things because they can, eh?"

Camaráin thought back to Lord Saibhir, and all the trouble he had put Uncle Iósaf through, just for his own vanity. He looked down at Brían, the hatchling evidently bored and curling up on the floor, eyes focused on the books ahead. He could very well have still been left unhatched on a shelf somewhere in Saibhir's mansion had he and Ailís not rescued the eggs. Suffice it to say, he was fully aware of powerful people doing whatever they wanted and nodded to Una's comment.

"Maybe the Priory does it because it can. Maybe they just want their ban of fae scholarship to actually have meaning. Frankly, I think the High Prior himself has lost sight of why the Priory wanted to do away with the fae in the first place. Who's to say?" Una shrugged, letting loose a sigh. "All I can say for sure is, these hunters they've brought in...they're bad news, the lot of them."

"Just who are they, if not the Inquisition with a different purpose?" Áine asked. Her face was stern; she seemed the most concerned out of all of them.

"They call themselves…" Una paused, rolling her eyes. "The Fae Smashers."

Camaráin stifled a laugh but stopped himself.

"Go ahead and laugh. Their name is ridiculous. And I'm hardly the only one who thinks so."

"What a holy group of merry men for the Priory to bring in," Ma murmured.

"Tell me about it. They've had some questionable names in the past but every once in a while feel the need to change it. They actually put the group name to a committee! Can you believe that?" Una threw her hands up in the air, shaking her head. "They don't even 'smash' fae, anyway! All they do is capture and imprison them. Now, they're trying to create this image of the super-strong warrior-hunters of yore, but all they do is come across as edgy, stupid, inbre—"

"Um," Áine raised a hand, cutting her off. "You seem more irate toward their name rather than, you know, what they actually *do*. Can we move this along?"

"Huh?" Una stopped mid-stride, lowering her hands back to her hips. "Right, sorry. They changed their name about a week or two ago and it's still bugging me."

Ma scoffed, a slight smirk on her lips. "Meanwhile, all this time, the Inquisition couldn't be bothered to shorten their name after however many generations."

On the floor, Brían snorted. Either he was agreeing with Ma about the Inquisition's ineptitude, or he was just bored. It could have been both.

"Regardless, whatever the…" Una sighed, rolling her eyes again. "…Fae Smashers' aim is, one thing seems clear: they're trying to goad the fae into doing something stupid to justify another Inquisition for the Priory."

Camaráin gasped. "That's horrible!" He held his dragon close to his chest, much to Brían's chagrin. The hatchling swung his legs, trying desperately to reach the ground, but to no avail. "The Priory can't just—"

"Relax, Camaráin," Una interrupted. "It won't happen. These people are too short-sighed to do anything other than hunt for sport, and the fae have made their living by being too mischievous and intelligent for humans to handle. I wouldn't worry about something like that happening again."

Silence hung in the air for a few seconds too long. Áine leaned in, raising her brow, and said, "I think you forgot to say, 'But...'"

Una snapped and pointed at her. "You're right, I did." She cleared her throat. "But..."

"Just get on with it."

"You've met one of these Fae Smashers before."

"The man who captured the faerie that Brían was chasing. Yeah, I figured that much out already." Áine crossed her arms and shrugged her shoulders. "What of it?"

Una puffed out her cheeks and exhaled a long breath, concern and irritation plastered across her face. "His name is Robeárd. A real cruel sort, that one. As a whole, I'm not too worried about the Fae Smashers, but this guy, it goes without saying he kinda scares me. Word gets around that his cruelty isn't reserved solely for the fae he captures."

That sent a chill down Camaráin's spine. He used to be intimidated by the Inquisitors, but generally only because of how much taller they were than he. Once the mask of their authority had been ripped off, he realized there was nothing of them to fear. But if this Robeárd was as cruel as Una said he was, he had only to hope he'd never bump into him. Or, at the least, he'd be able to hide behind a book until the hunter left under the hope he had no sense of object permanence.

"You're saying this guy is someone we need to worry about," Áine said. "Not just for the sake of the fae."

"For now," Una said, "let's save it for just the fae. And for Brían as well."

The dragon turned his head toward Una, an inquisitive glint in his eyes.

Camaráin mimed the reaction. "Why? What do they want with Brían?"

Áine stepped forward. "You mentioned a selkie that would be happy to meet with the dragon. What does Brían have to do with any of this?"

Sighing, Una looked at the hatchling, worry evident in her eyes. "The selkie is the Priory's—or, I should say, the Fae Smashers'—next quarry. They're soon to move out to the shores to hunt her."

"How are you so sure?"

"It made for a riveting sermon during mass the other day."

"Oh, good Lord."

"I wouldn't go that far, but yes."

"Selkies are elusive, though," Áine said. "How can you—or they, for that matter—be sure one exists to begin with?"

Una outturned her hands, as though the answer was obvious. "I've met her."

"Okay." Áine crossed her arms, furrowing her brow. "So, it's personal for you? You don't want them to hunt a friend? Then, why are we involved?"

"I wouldn't call us 'friends,' per se. Acquaintances, maybe? Regardless, you are more involved than you realize."

"Obviously. That's why I keep asking you questions."

"Oh, right."

Áine rolled her eyes. "Make with the answers."

An exasperated sigh left Una's lips. "Because any pain brought to that selkie will hurt Brían as well." The words seem to pain her just the same.

Camaráin took a step back, clutching Brían tighter. "What do you mean? What does a selkie want with him?"

"What else?" Una threw her hands out at her side. "To bring him home."

"'Home?'" Camaráin repeated, anger slipping into his voice. "Home is with me and Ma, back in Baile!"

Una looked away. "Not quite."

"Fine, then the Highlands, if we want to get specific about it."

"No, Camaráin." Una's face was touched with what looked to be genuine sadness. "Not the Highlands, either."

His arms shaking, Camaráin looked down at Brían, who looked as though he, too, knew the truth of the matter already. "What...what are you saying?"

"I'm saying," Una began, looking at the ground, "that the selkie is well aware of Brían's hatching. She felt it the moment it happened. Because he's not of the Draconic Highlands. He's not Bonded to you. He's Bonded to her.

"He's faebound."

Turns out Brían wasn't half-gnome after all.

Chapter Fifteen

The word hung in the air, echoing in Camaráin's head over and over again. He stared at Brían, the dragon sparing not a single glance in his direction. Whether it was due to shock, or shame at knowing his fate, or simple disdain toward the boy for thinking he had the right to a Bond with him, Camaráin could not say. All that remained plain, regardless of the wordless exchange between he and the dragon, was that single word that rang in his head.

Faebound.

"That's just...not possible," he muttered, sitting cross-legged on the ground next to Brían. He had cared for the dragon's egg, kept it safe, saved it from the clutches of Lord Saibhir and the smuggler, hid it from the Inquisition. They had bonded, even if they did not share a Bond proper. Brían displayed a curiousness toward books and knowledge, just as Camaráin had. Why was the Bond not his? It wasn't right. He looked at Áine. "Right? It's not possible, Áine, right? You know everything there is to know about dragons. He should be Bonded to me!"

Áine did not answer straight away. A frown creased her lips, her arms crossed, forefinger tapping against her elbow as though she was deep in thought. She kept her eyes averted from Camaráin's.

That was the wrong answer. "Áine?" Camaráin said, tears welling in his eyes. "Tell me! It's not possible!"

Sighing, Áine looked to the ground and said, "All I needed was the confirmation. I'm sorry, Cam."

His jaw dropped, his hand reaching toward Brían, whose own head hung low. The dragon inched away from Camaráin's touch, the heat cast from his scales drawing further from him. He couldn't help but feel betrayed at the revelation, and his first instinct was to cast angry eyes at Una. "How could you let this happen?"

Una shrugged. "How's it *my* fault? I didn't expect dragons to still exist until a few days ago. You shouldn't just assume that—"

"Don't." Ma extended a hand to quiet her. She sighed as she looked at her son, a genuine sadness coloring her face. "Our family has been living in interesting times enough already these last few weeks. Don't make it worse, please."

Though she opened her mouth to speak further, Una took the advice and quieted herself.

Ma cast her glare at Áine. "You knew, didn't you? All this time?"

Áine still averted her eyes, looking instead to the collection of tomes held within this hidden library, to the researchers lurking about in the background, going about their business and pretending a family crisis was not currently ongoing in their presence. "Never claim to know something without proof. I needed the confirmation, and I got it."

"Ever the scholar, you." Ma's tone did not seem to be one of appreciation.

"What does a selkie want with a dragon to begin with, Una?"

Áine asked, looking at the fae researcher. "The last I knew, the only 'bonds' they sought were with unsuspecting men whom they enthralled with their singing. Maybe they're kindred spirits with us in that sense, but I haven't made a habit of Bonding with dragons on the side."

"I don't know," Una said. "That's not for me to know."

"You research the fae. That's probably *exactly* for you to know."

"Hmph, really. Then I assume you know everything there is to know about dragons, Priest?"

"I thought you said the people of Mór never used sarcasm."

"I did. It was a genuine question."

"You're insufferable."

"Most researchers are. Wouldn't you agree?"

Una's colleagues mumbled in response, confusion plain on the faces of a couple of them, perhaps unsure at being called "insufferable." An unaware and insufferable lot, them.

Wanting nothing to do with a discussion of what researchers did and did not know, Camaráin made his way to the bookshelves, hoping, praying that some book would hold the answer he was looking for, that everything he did in protection and service to Brían's egg wasn't for naught. His attention caught first to the shelves labeled *Scholarly*, where he found books with titles such as *All's Fae in Love and War*; *Three Hundred Centuries of Questions: The Fae, and the Answers We May Never Find*; and, *Herbie: Faely Loaded*, but quick skims through what he could reach found him nothing of use, and much he could not understand. The adjacent section labeled *Propaganda* offered even less of value, with books such as *The Fae Agenda* and *Gnomes Blew Up My Couch but It Got Better* spouting nothing but poorly researched nonsense intended only to inflame and anger.

The more he looked, the more he realized that scholarship was not finding the answers that proved him right, but rather finding the answers that largely made him depressed.

His heart skipped a beat when he came across the *New-found Scholarship* section and, more importantly, a subsection marked *Dragons*. Camaráin rushed over to the shelf, filled with a riveting collection of no more than four books, and no less than three, but titles such as *The Story Yet Unwritten: Three Weeks of Draconic Scholarship* and *Flights of Fancy: The Rise and Fall and Crash and Burn of an Airline Industry Ahead of its Time* did little to instill confidence or excitement.

The final book on the shelf very well was the final nail in the coffin. He picked it up, his hands shaking as he read the gold lettering embossed on the spine that said, *For the Benefit of Dragon and Fae: The Brighter Tomorrow and a Worrisome Past*. Camaráin opened it, dreading what was penned inside.

There was nothing.

"Oh, come on," he groaned.

"Sorry, boss," one of the researchers said behind him. "That one'll be a while."

Camaráin turned around. "Did you spend all this time writing the title on the spine?"

The researcher shrugged. "Beats actually writing the book."

Apparently, scholarship was also an exercise in the art of procrastination.

Placing the book back on the shelf, Camaráin solemnly dug his hands into his pockets and walked back to the group, all of whom watched him with equivalent silence. Áine and Una stared at one another, Ma and Granma seemed to be putting on their most encouraging faces for his benefit, and Brían...

For all his attitude and annoyance since they journeyed down south, the dragon appeared upset. He refused to lift his head, refused to glance in Camaráin's direction. It had to count for something.

"It still doesn't make sense, Una," Áine said, breaking the silence.

"What doesn't?" Una asked.

"How did Brían's egg make it this far south to begin with? And who brought it back to the north? It was smuggled out of the Highlands with another egg at the same time."

Una flashed her teeth noncommittally. "I don't know, Áine. Truly, I don't." She looked at Camaráin, an unspoken apology seeming to glint in her eyes, and then redirected her attention to Brían. "All I can say for certain, is that this dragon is going to be the key to getting the selkie to safety. And the longer we dilly-dally, the more danger she's in. The hunt is soon to begin."

"I don't suppose you know a thing or two about outwitting and outlasting hunters?"

"If I did, Áine, I wouldn't be spending all my time in a basement."

Áine shrugged. "Worth a shot."

Worth it indeed, so far as Camaráin was concerned. For he knew that the longer they dilly-dallied, the longer he'd get to continue enjoying Brían's company. For what it was worth.

Brían began to snore.

For what it was worth indeed.

Chapter Sixteen

T he cathedral's cellar always carried with it a musty odor. The last time Robeárd had raised the issue, he was told an assortment of things ranging from, "What would a hunter know of cleanliness?" to "Verse 7, line 9 of the Book of Bob-on-High states, 'Let he who doth smelt it, be he who hath dealt it,'" to "Look, buddy, we just don't have enough money to hire cleaners when all our money is going toward the first megapriory in the land." He could never be certain which was the real answer, so he resolved never to bring it up again.

It didn't help matters that, for all the extravagance of the nave upstairs, the cellar looked more like a dungeon. It was damp, poorly lit, the stone walls and flooring stained with water, and the only furnishing was a row of metal folding chairs where he sat amongst his comrades.

To the credit of the High Prior, at least, he sat in the same cheap chairs, which contrasted with the garish robes of rich fabrics and gold lining, and the hat tall enough to hide a basket of figs atop his head. The head of the Priory wiped the fig juice trickling from the corner of his mouth and extended his arms toward Robeárd and his crew.

"You have my gratitude for meeting like this before we begin," he said, his throat still hoarse from the day's sermon.

"But of course, Your Holiness," Robeárd said, bowing his head. "You said it was a matter of utmost urgency."

The High Prior bowed his head in return and made the sign of the Thrice-Dead Prophet, in which he held both hands parallel to his head, and smacked his own cheeks three times. "It is, indeed."

"Then, please proceed, Your Righteousness. Is there something we need to know of the selkie before we embark?"

"There is a more pressing matter that I believe we must resolve first."

Robeárd raised his brow. "Oh?"

Clasping his hands, the High Prior upturned his chin and asked, "Is there not something we can do about the name?"

"...The name?"

"Of your...band of merry men."

Robeárd looked to his comrades on either side, exchanging tepid glances with them. "What is wrong with our name?"

"Well..." The High Prior stopped to give the sign of the Prophet once more—*smacksmacksmack*—and eyed Robeárd with a glint in his eyes. "The name is quite stupid."

Shooting to his feet, knocking his chair to the ground, Robeárd pointed at the High Prior. "How dare you! We workshopped the name for weeks!"

"It *was* the best we came up with, Your Magnanimousness," admitted one of his comrades in a meek voice.

"But we don't have to *tell* him that!" Robeárd flashed a sneer at the man, but there was precious little else he could do when it was the truth. "We really shouldn't have fired that guy who gave us our names. Two days away from retirement," he muttered, shaking his head.

"Oh," the High Prior said. *Smacksmacksmack.* "What happened to him?"

"He took an early retirement."

"I see. A shame he didn't wait until after giving you a better name than Fae Smashers."

Robeárd clenched his fists. "That's *not* how it works, Your God-Talkingness. Every time someone leaves the group, we need to rebrand. New members, new name, *that's* the rule!"

"For all the funds we provide, you could perhaps put it toward a creative consultant?" *Smacksmacksmack.*

With a sigh, Robeárd hung his head and said, "That would mean we'd need another new name."

"Good. Maybe it will be one that sticks. Now, please sit, Robeárd." The High Prior gestured toward the upturned chair and the hunter obliged. "Now, then. Once this matter with the selkie is handled, I will ensure your next onboarding will be for one who will give you a name with no reference to inane...*smashing*. You are still in the employ of the Prophet." *Smasksmacksmack.*

"Yes, Your Prophetness." A shame. Robeárd was quite proud of the name Fae Smashers.

"Good. With that out of the way, shall we get to the business of the matter? Have you a plan in place for this selkie?"

Robeárd nodded. He felt a spring return to his step, contentment returning as he leaned back in his chair, crossing one leg over the other, black leather creaking as he bent his knee. "Yes, we do. The woods shall be our ally in this endeavor. One of us shall act as bait to draw the creature out of the water and lead it to the forest. There, the rest of us shall lie in wait, ready to strike. Come dawn, the issue of the selkie shall be no more."

Smacksmacksmack. "Excellent," the High Prior said, tapping his fingertips together. "Your confidence is ever appreciated, Robeárd. I trust you will ensure this selkie does, indeed, take the bait? It was to my understanding they are loath to leave the water."

The other Fae Smashers stayed quiet. Some tapped their feet, others hummed a tuneless melody to themselves. Another was fast asleep, snoring away.

But Robeárd maintained that same confident smile he had adopted the moment plans were being discussed. He reveled in the hunt, longed for it, dreamt of it, thought about it while cooking his meals, and tended to bring it up on most romantic engagements that never lasted the entire evening. He was certain of this plan. "It will all work out, Your Faetredness. Come the dawn, that selkie will be in a cage for whatever you want to do with it."

The High Prior reached into his hat and withdrew another fig, taking a large bite from it. "There have never been greater words spoken in my presence."

"Really? Because aren't you, I don't know, a man of faith? Aren't those words you read during your sermons greater than...ah never mind, forget about it. The usual payment arrangement, then?"

Juice spilling out from his mouth, the High Prior nodded and said, "One steak dinner now, and all your worthless baubles later."

Robeárd shot back to his feet, gesturing to his comrades. "Then come, lads! I wish to peruse the collection baskets before we depart."

Chapter Seventeen

I t was the closest Camaráin had ever been to the ocean. Well, scratch that. He had been quite near the water while journeying through the Cliffs of Ard, but to touch the ocean at that point probably only would have happened after a painful fall, and no one wanted that.

So, it was the closest Camaráin had ever been to the ocean, so long as being able to touch the water didn't require jumping off a cliff, which was much more mother-tested and mother-approved.

Una had led them out of Mór and to the southern shores, the light fading over the horizon, the water glimmering with the golden rays of the setting sun largely in Camaráin's imagination—the ocean did hardly anything in view of the cloud-covered sky. Small waves broke and crashed with the evening tide, the water gliding against a sandy shoreline peppered with shells, sea glass, and the trousers of no fewer than three longshoremen.

The walk south was done mostly in silence, save for the vocal direction given by Una once they left the city. The sting of betrayal had not yet left Camaráin's heart, and the expression of shame was still evident upon Brían's serpentine face. The dragon had crawled into Camaráin's bag some time ago and did not raise a stink about it, instead nestling into a place of comfort and sighing himself to sleep (either feigned or genuine). Though Camaráin felt attempts at comfort alternating between a gentle hand from Ma, hugs from Granma, and words of encouragement from Áine, it did little to lessen the hurt. He wished it was as easy as it was for Granda and Cousin Gnome when they reconciled, but at this point, he didn't think throwing a hat on Brían's head and going to the pub would do much good, largely because, at the age of eight, he was rarely allowed within a pub's doors.

And now, they waited at Una's suggestion, though for what, he could not say. His bag left open to allow Brían to breathe, Camaráin ran his fingers through the loose grains of sand, avoiding the sand on the other side of his body that was rougher and more painful. The coarse sand felt akin to running his hand the opposite way up Brían's back rather than with the flow of his scales. There was a metaphor there, but Camaráin had never learned what metaphors were, so he did not raise the connection.

Silence carried on well after the last of the light disappeared to the west, the sound of the crashing waves the only voice given to the scene. When Camaráin had first learned that they were going to visit Granma and Granda, he could hardly have guessed this was where he would be only a week or so later, covered in sand, his Bond stripped from him, and the books in which he had long found comfort providing only misfortune.

All for the sake of a selkie who he would never have sought out under normal circumstances. More and more, despite promising Ma this would be a different story, he wished his adventure with Brían was more like the one Ailís got to experience with Pilib.

Despite it all, a scholarly curiosity gripped him. Despite the frustration given to him by the answers, he still felt compelled by the questions. If there was anything this journey had taught Camaráin, it was that being a scholar was both a blessing and a curse. More so a curse; the blessings were fleeting. But, regardless of the curse that may have resulted from the answer, the blessing lay in the question as he turned toward Una. "Why is protecting this selkie so important to you? The fae are too scary, and, if I could, I would just avoid them forever."

Folding her knees up to her chest, Una wrapped her arms around her legs and offered a gentle smile to the boy. "I suppose I'm not unlike the fae. I always found greater kinship with them than I ever did with people."

Camaráin inclined his head toward her, puzzled. "What do you mean? You live in the capital and there are lots of people there. Why wouldn't you leave Mór if you didn't like anyone there?"

With a chuckle, Una said, "It's not as easy as you think to just pack up and leave the only place I've ever called home. What do you expect of me—to live in the woods? That doesn't sound fun."

"I make do just fine," Áine said, her tone plain and matter-of-fact. "I prefer the company of fae to people just the same, and I've never found issue with my home."

"What about Uncle Iósaf?" Camaráin asked. "Wasn't he an issue?"

"Communicating with him with pies and an angry gnome as a go-between? Far from the biggest issue I've ever faced, Cam."

It was not lost on Camaráin the special attention Granma was giving to Áine's answer, but if there were any revelations from the interactions between her and Uncle Iósaf, it was clear they would go no deeper than that, at which point Granma redirected her gaze to the ocean instead.

Turning back toward Una, Camaráin asked, "Even if you don't want to live with them in the woods, they must mean a lot to you, right?"

The young researcher dug her heels into the sand, the sea breeze blowing tufts of her dark hair in front of her eyes. "Growing up, I was a bit of a loner," she began. "I didn't have many friends—scratch that, I didn't have *any* friends. My parents passed due to illness when I was very young, and I spent most of my childhood years at an orphanage run by the Priory. Most children don't want to play with an orphan because they think them to be strange or poor or smelly. In my case, they were correct, but they didn't have to *say* all that. The other children at the orphanage wanted little to do with me as well, probably because I found more enjoyment in reading the Priory-sanctioned stories they provided us that had most of the words scribbled out—my favorite was a story called *The ~~Heroic Adventures of Ardal the~~ Fae, ~~the Evil-Slaying Champion~~*—rather than playing stickball or stick-swords or stick-economics or whatever stick-based limited activities the Priory provided us.

"It also didn't help that the orphanage was dreadfully boring. Every day was the same routine: waking up, cleaning the cathedral, eating our meals, having the fear of the Lord guilted into us, and posing for advertisements for the orphanage. As I got older, I learned that we should have been financially compensated for our work, but child labor laws weren't put into effect until about six weeks ago here. At least I received back-pay for my work, which may also be why the Priory has been more forceful with the collection baskets of late." She shrugged. "Not for me to know how to run a religion."

In the distance, the Priory's bells rang, signaling the turn of the next hour. From this far away, it was finally not piercing Camaráin's eardrums.

"Anyway," Una continued, "One day, I found a page of a book that the Priory seemed to have accidentally skipped over that ran counter to everything else I had read and was also much more coherent. For the longest time, I thought I was horrible at reading, but it turns out I only have the Priory to blame."

"The pages of crossed-out words weren't enough of a hint for you?" Áine asked.

"Grow up with those being your first books and maybe then you'll understand," Una responded, sneering at the Draconic Priest. "Anyway, I read that there were fae in the woods south of the city, and though my afternoons were meant to be spent signing contracts to use my likeness in newsletters, Priory plays, and recipe books, I would often sneak away to go on adventures in the woods. Even when the Priory found out, all they would say was that they wished I wouldn't do that, or they'd recite the thirty-ninth commandment of 'Thou shalt not consort with they who flitter and glitter and get all mischievous with us,' or they'd give me a stern talking-to that I didn't read the fine print of my thirteenth contract. I didn't care; none of that mattered to me.

"All it took was a single trip to the woods to learn that there was nothing to fear. The fae I encountered weren't evil by any means. All they wanted was to coexist with us. All they *still* want is to coexist with us." Una paused, watching Brían slowly crawling out of Camaráin's bag. "I'd assume you can empathize with that much, having recently had your own run-ins with the Inquisition."

Camaráin hesitated to bring his hand to Brían's head, but the dragon looked at him, flashing none of the arrogance or annoyance he had been of late. Though his heart remained heavy, he still allowed himself to run his hand down the dragon's scaled neck. Brían trilled his approval, though with muted enthusiasm.

Áine nodded along to Una's point. If ever there was someone who had had "run-ins" with the Inquisition, it was her.

"Any subject worth being banned is a subject worth investigating just *why* it's banned," Una continued. "Perhaps that's just my scholar's brain speaking. And I still cannot understand the bone the Priory has picked with the fae other than wanting to have something to fear. But, part of being a scholar is having a specialty in something many people have no desire to understand. It's quite the lonely existence, that."

Hearing that made Camaráin's heart sink. All the stories he had read growing up, either via Uncle Iósaf or through his own curiosity, had made him consider the path of a scholar. The last few days had opened his eyes to the fact that the path of the scholar kind of sucked.

"So...that's why, Camaráin," Una said. "This selkie is important to me because I understand her. I understand what it is to be misunderstood and isolated. It's because of the Priory that the fae relegate themselves to the remote regions of Nóra, away from the leering eyes of humans—"

"They're really not a problem up north," Áine muttered.

"—and if there's one thing that I can spend my life doing, it's ensuring that they are better understood. If I can help one person learn contrary to the Priory's teachings, that would be enough."

Camaráin continued to pat Brían's neck in silence, considering Una's words. As the waves broke in the distance, he added, "Doesn't that sound a waste of time to only change one person's mind your whole life?"

"Camaráin!" Ma exclaimed.

"No, he's right," Una said, her voice lowering. "But I've spent too much time and energy toward this career to change now."

"What?" Áine's face scrunched together in confusion. "You say that like you've wasted your whole life. How old are you again?"

"Nineteen."

Her eyes bulging, Áine stammered before saying, "You're ten years younger than I am—you realize you have you have plenty of time to change your career, right?"

Una was quick to shake her head. "In Mór, they make you choose your intended career when you're eight years old, at which point you better pray you were right about what you wanted to do. It's not so much having the time to change as it is facing the exorbitant financial costs to reeducate myself."

Áine buried her face in her hands and muttered into her palms, "What is wrong with this city?"

Ignoring Áine's distaste for the city of Mór, Una added, "If ever there was one group whose mind I *could* change, though, it'd be those Fae Smashers. The Priory regards the fae with fear, the general population with ignorance, my colleagues with fascination. But these hunters...it's all just sport to them, and that feels most wrong of all. In using them, the Priory wants to 'fix' the land, but all they have is a hammer."

A sharp sound broke the night sky, a chill running down Camaráin's spine as though he were within earshot of the cathedral's bells. But this was not the Priory's insistence on being overly loud. It was something else.

The sound of trumpets.

Una smacked her lips. "And the hammer now wishes to smash."

Chapter Eighteen

There wasn't a moment to lose. Una jumped to her feet and sprinted for the shore, kicking up sand with each step. Camaráin followed, scooping Brían in his arms and sprinting away from the sound of trumpets, the others close behind.

Turning his head over his shoulder, he shouted, "I'm sorry, Ma!"

A perplexed expression overtook Ma's face. "What for?"

"I said this story would be different, but I didn't want it to be *this* different!"

"Camaráin, what are you talking about?"

"Never mind, I'll explain later!"

The footing was poor, and Camaráin could barely keep his balance while chasing after Una, who ran as though she had done this before, which, if he could read Áine's mind, was probably another thing to blame the city of Mór for.

His heart pounded by the time he caught up to the scholar, who had stopped just short of the water. A fervor had gripped Una, her head turning one way and then the next in quick succession, as though there was anything to see in the black of night. She tapped her foot in the sand, impatience evident, rapping her knuckles against her hip, until finally she cupped her hands over her mouth and shouted, "Nil!"

"Nil?" Camaráin repeated. "The selkie has a name?"

Una turned to him, her brow furrowed. "Everyone has a name, Camaráin. Even me."

Slowly, he nodded. "I know. It's Una."

"Exactly." She looked back to the sea and shouted the selkie's name several times more, her voice echoing more the louder she screamed. When no response came, she gritted her teeth and cursed. It was a word Camaráin recognized, but that he was forbidden from ever repeating, so he put it out of his mind.

"No luck?" Áine called, finally having caught up with Una and Camaráin. "No idea how you managed to run that fast in sand. We kept falling over."

"Well, that's what happens when you lose your youth."

"Watch yourself, now," Granma warned, pointing at Una.

"You used sarcasm!" Camaráin exclaimed, a smile on his face that he wasn't expecting.

Una raised an eyebrow. "I did what now?"

"Oh. Never mind."

Ma stepped forward, placing a gentle hand on Camaráin's shoulder to get him to back away. "What are we to look for here?" she asked.

Una frowned and shook her head. "I don't know, anything."

"Thanks, that's helpful."

"Just call her name. Sooner or later, she'll emerge."

The group took the instructions to heart, everyone shouting Nil's name into the night, though it sounded like Granma was saying, "Wil" instead. Given the circumstances, Camaráin hoped the selkie wouldn't be too offended by the mispronunciation.

All the while, Brían started to fidget more and more in Camaráin's grasp. The hatchling batted at his arms with wings spread wide, straining at the effort to pry himself loose from the boy's clutches.

"Ow! Brían!" Camaráin shouted. "You're not helping here!"

Brían continued to not help by swatting with his wings some more, knocking his head against Camaráin's hands, until finally, he took a quick bite of the boy's index finger, not enough to draw blood, but just enough for the grip to loosen and for him to drop to the ground, landing in a puff of sand.

Shaking his hand at the sudden jab, Camaráin looked at the dragon and yelled, "What was that for?"

Having no clear inclination to answer—largely because he had no capacity to speak—Brían spared not a single glance back at Camaráin, and instead sprinted for the sea, past everyone who could do no more than watch with confusion, then with concern, then with more confusion, and then with disbelief as this hatchling dragon, lacking the capacity yet to fly...dove into the ocean, his form gone in a flash.

The calls for Nil the selkie ceased as they all looked at one another, wondering if they were all imagining things. The same things. The same obscure, unbelievable things.

Camaráin dropped to his knees, his mouth agape, eyes welling with tears. "Áine?" he said. "Do dragons swim?"

"I don't see why they would ever need to, Cam, given they *fly*," Áine answered, perhaps more snide than she intended. She still seemed annoyed by Una and the general insanity of the city of Mór.

Finding not the strength to return to his feet, Camaráin

crawled to where the tide broke, staring blankly into the dark depths of the sea. He could hear Ma's approach, a comforting hand looming, Granma's soothing voice offering assurances that it would be okay. But he cared not to hear them. All he could focus on was the gentle crashing of the waves in front of him, and the dragon they swallowed.

If only he could have also focused on the rush of water that was heading right for his face. He never could avoid that prank; it was a favorite of his sister's. Either way, he had been sad, and now he was sad and drenched, which was generally the worst time to be sad.

By the time he wiped the sea water from his eyes, his nose was assaulted by the odor of low tide (which smelled just like Baile) his tongue peppered with the flavors of the sea (very similar to the mud of Baile) and off to the side, he could hear Una stifling her laughter (very little like the people of Baile, who would not try to hide their laughter at another's expense). He opened his mouth to either say something or let loose the wail of an unfortunate boy in the wrong place at the wrong time, but he was interrupted by Una's splashing footsteps and excited voice.

"Nil!" she exclaimed.

The seawater stung at his eyes, but Camaráin still managed to focus just enough to take in the form wading in the shallow water before him: a slender woman, her body a combination of flesh and scales, damp hair the color of fire clinging to her shoulders and down to her waist, facial features so ordinary save for her eyes, wide and bulging like those of a fish.

And on her shoulder...the unfurled wings of a young dragon, droplets of seawater cascading back into the ocean.

"Nil," Una said again, a relieved chuckle coloring her breath. "I'm so happy we found you in time."

The selkie, Nil, waded closer to Una, her body dipping below the water in the approach. A second glance revealed to Camaráin that the lower half of her body resembled a fish's fin.

"Una," Nil said, setting her long hands on the researcher's shoulders and placing a kiss on her brow. Her voice was calm and melodic, in stark contrast to the loud and abrasive trumpets that continued to blare in the distance. "I cannot begin to thank you enough for bringing him back to me." She looked at her shoulder, where Brían sat perched with head held high, all the troubles of a short while ago having seemingly disappeared. "I could feel his entry into this world from the moment he hatched all those weeks ago. I wish only to have seen him sooner."

Wringing out his shirt with a snarl on his face, Camaráin rose to his feet and said, "First, are you hiding a towel somewhere down there? And second, Brían is *my* dra—"

Una extended an arm in front of him and shook her head. "There'll be time enough for that later, Camaráin." She shot her gaze to Nil. "We need to hide her before the Fae Smashers arrive. Come along, Nil, we can—"

Nil rose her hand, and Una immediately quieted. "Pardon the interruption, Una, but did you say the 'Fae Smashers?' They wouldn't happen to be..."

Nodding, Una grunted. "They're the same."

"What would possess them to adopt such a stupid name? Their last name was...well, still ridiculous, but..."

The trumpets blared even louder. They were drawing near.

"We can talk about creative impotence later, Nil. For now,

we need to get away from here."

Nil slunk closer to the shore, her body taking on an ethereal glow. "Oh, there's no need to rush, Una. I can buy us a little more time." In a flash, the aquatic lower half of Nil's body changed shape, bearing the appearance of human legs, though still colored by the sea and marked with scales. She flexed her fingers, stepping past Camaráin and the rest of them, and peered at the dragon atop her shoulder. "Shall we begin?"

Brían turned his head toward Camaráin, his eyes lingering on the boy, until finally he turned back to Nil and held his head high. It almost looked like he nodded.

The selkie turned her head to the ground as she extended a long arm. "I would advise taking a few more steps back."

Camaráin was practically in the ocean already, but what more of a difference would it have made at that point, given how wet he was? He sat cross-legged and cross-armed as the tide came up to his hips.

With a smile, Nil returned her gaze northward, where trumpets blared and horses galloped in a show of stealth—not a good one, but still *a* show—and her hand began to radiate with a red-orange light. She took a deep breath, Brían unfurling his wings beside her, and as she exhaled, a rush of heat gathered in the immediate vicinity, almost oppressive. It pulled at Camaráin, nearly knocking him forward, the air growing thin and losing its warmth. Nil's hand glowed brighter and brighter until at last, the gathering heat took form in front of her palm. Tendrils of flame interlaced with one another, one after the other, joining together and uniting in a small sphere, embers sparking off of it.

And in a blink, Nil unflexed her fingers, and the sphere of fire shot forward. A wall of fire rose on the northern horizon just as quickly, and the abrasive trumpeters stopped, replaced instead with panicked cries and general finger-pointing over who had to put out the fire.

Camaráin felt a pit sinking in his stomach at the sight. It was all the confirmation he needed: Brían was not Bonded to him; he was Bonded to Nil. But, on the other hand...

"Ma," he said. "Maybe it's a good thing I didn't end up with a Bond with—"

"BELIEVE ME I KNOW LET'S NEVER SPEAK OF THIS AGAIN." From her bulging eyes and stark-white face, Ma must have been very happy about that.

Chapter Nineteen

As it turned out, the fae were capable of raining fire on people. Robeárd had read nothing on that in any of the field guides that he had written.

The horses reared and whinnied as the ground erupted before them, halting their advance before they could draw anywhere near the shore. For such rain-soaked ground, it really took to flame quickly. Already the wall of fire stood tall, blocking the Fae Smashers even from going around it. It was spreading inward, back toward the city.

Robeárd turned, seeing the eyes of some of his comrades bulging, others squinting, and one other maintaining the same expression he always had, though that was because he had lost both of his eyes when he mistook a lit candle for his eyebrow tweezer. Fate was funny like that sometimes.

Dismounting from his horse, Robéard growled and tried to look past the blaze, forgetting he had a better view atop his mount. "Blast it, the hunt can wait for now. This fire is already spreading. If it gets any worse, we're risking the city burning down."

"We can't let that happen!" one of the hunters shouted. "Especially after the last capital burned down because of that gender reveal party!"

"Right, whose bright idea was it to hold it next to the powder stores when they were revealing the gender with an *explosive*?" A second hunter shook his head in disbelief.

"Didn't that baby end up owning a mansion up north?"

"I think he's a *governor* up north."

"Heard he went missing, though."

"Heard the Inquisition had a field day at his mansion, only to find out they lost their jobs an hour later."

"Life's funny, ain't it?"

"Quite so. My arm hurts." A sleeve catching fire will do that.

Robeárd rolled his eyes. "Are you quite done, lads? Go get some water to douse the flames!"

While the inflamed hunter took to rolling on the ground, the others dug their hands in their pockets.

"What?" Robeárd demanded. "Trying to find water in your pockets, are you?"

"Boss, we didn't bring any water with us," admitted a hunter far from the flames—smart lad, that one. "You said thirsty work ain't work worth doing."

"Quicker we can get done is quicker we can get drinking, you said," added another.

"No water near us 'cept for the sea, too," said another.

"And we can't get to the sea without runnin' through the fire, boss!"

The wall spat out sparkling embers, frightening the horses into scampering away largely unmanned, save for the one hunter whose heel was caught in the stirrup. Hanging upside down, he shouted to his comrades as he was dragged along, "Tell my wife I always hated fish and chips! She'll know what it means!" as his voice faded over the horizon.

Despite the flames licking his shoulders, Robeárd stood in place, shaking his head in disbelief. "Fine!" He reached to the two closest hunters and grabbed them both by the collar, hurling them both over the blazing wall. "No going *through* the flames—you happy?!"

On the other side of the fire, one of the Fae Smashers shouted, "We don't have anything to carry the water over! All we've got is our helmets!"

"Then there you go! Get to it!" Robeárd looked with frustration at who he had left on this side of the flames: the man still rolling on the ground, the fire long since doused, so it was likely he just liked the feeling of grass; three men with hands in their pockets, evidently still trying to find water within them; and the man with no eyes, who somehow looked the most competent of the bunch. He didn't envision this being a difficult evening by any means. He was looking forward to being back in bed at this point. But now?

"Well," he said, kicking at the ground, "there's not much else we can do except wait around for the fire to be put out. Or put out enough, at least."

"Wish we brought some snacks," said one of the hunters.

"Or some cards," added another.

"Cards would catch fire here."

"Cards can catch fire anywhere—they're made of *paper*."

"Anyone have any water? I'm getting thirsty."

"Sorry, my pocket water's run out."

Robeárd turned, clasping his hands behind his back, allowing the inane conversations to carry on. He looked ahead to the horizon, but the horizon was on fire, and that was inconvenient. It hurt his eyes to look at it.

Aloud, he wondered, "How in the world does a faerie horse make fire like this? The High Prior best be paying us double for our troubles here."

The conversations of his men quieted, and they took to whispering amongst themselves, seeming to discuss Robeárd's thoughts. He couldn't pick up most of what they were saying, but he did hear the word, "kelpie" thrown around a few times.

Why they were talking about seaweed at a time like this was beyond him, but hunger could bring a man to strange thoughts at strange times.

The first splash of water hit the flames and did very little. The second evaporated before even getting the opportunity.

Looked like they'd be here for a while.

Chapter Twenty

Watching two Fae Smashers stumbling through the sand with seawater in their helmets was entertaining, to say the least. It was enough to distract Camaráin from the raging fire. It reminded him of the *Lizard Wizard* series he read when he was younger, where no one ever raised any issue with any environmental damage caused by the hero and all would be forgotten and forgiven the next day. It always felt like lazy writing to him.

None of the adults were paying any mind to the fire, though. As they squatted at the edge of the woods, illuminated by faerielight, they were all far too preoccupied with the presence of the selkie, and the dragon alongside her. Nil maintained her human transformation, resting atop her knees, Brían sitting alert to her left. Camaráin was looking for anything *but* her to look at. Luckily, there was plenty to keep him occupied outside the woods.

"The boy is upset," Nil said, her voice lilting. "Is something the matter?"

Camaráin crossed his arms and turned his head over his shoulder, pulling himself away from the evening's entertainment. He still averted his eyes from the selkie but could not stop himself from staring at Brían. For his part, the dragon opted to look away as well, his head downturned as though in shame.

"Tinaeron? What's the matter?" Nil's long fingers scratched along the back of the dragon's head.

His nostrils flaring, Camaráin gritted his teeth, pointed an angry finger, and said, "His name isn't—wait, did you say Tinaeron?" He looked at Ma. "See? It's not so dumb a name now, is it?"

Ma inclined her head toward Nil. "Focus, Cam. Weren't you trying to be angry?"

"Oh, right." He furrowed his brow again. "His name is *Brían*! Not Tinaeron, even though that's a perfectly fine name for a dragon!" Taking a step forward, he reached out to the dragon. "Come on, Brían, tell her. You can do that, can't you?"

Brían glanced at Camaráin from the corner of his eyes, but just as quickly looked at the dirt, scratching at it with his claws.

A curious frown creased Nil's face, lifting her hand from the dragon's head and moving it toward her own chin. "Una, would you be a dear and fill me in on what is happening right now? I had thought we had an understanding."

"And I understood loud and clear, but how was I to know?" Una shrugged, glancing first at the dragon and then at Camaráin.

"What understanding?" Ma asked, grabbing her son's shoulder before he pounced forward. "I hope you haven't been lying to us, Una."

"You're with the Inquisition, aren't you?" Camaráin growled at her. "I should have known that—"

"You really think these two are with the Inquisition, Cam?"

Áine said. "That'd make for a cheap surprise. Believe me, I am more acquainted with those wannabe knights than any of you, so I have it on good authority to say that Una is far too competent to be an Inquisitor."

Una's squinted her eyes with confusion. "Thank you?"

"And the selkie would just confuse them far too much to permit her in their ranks; they prefer the simple, single-minded sort, and she's not that."

"Guilty as charged," Nil said with a smile.

"So," Áine continued, "we know that Una was looking for Brían. We know that Nil is Bonded to him. I can only assume that Una was tasked with bringing him to her. Is that the understanding?"

Una smacked her lips and shrugged half-heartedly. "That's about the size of it." Glancing at the selkie, she added, "I can't take the credit for bringing the dragon back to you, Nil. Sorry about that."

"Why are you saying you're bringing him *back* to her?" Camaráin shouted. Tears of frustration welled in his eyes, his hands balling into shaking fists. "*I* was the one who found his egg—"

"'Stole' the egg?" Ma chimed in, her tone deadpan.

"*Rescued* the egg!" Camaráin pouted, the issue of whether Pilib and Brían were "stolen" or "rescued" seemingly already settled on the last journey. "I had his egg with me the entire time we went to the Highlands! I kept him safe! I waited and waited for him to hatch! So why does she get to say she's taking him *back* when he was never hers to begin with?!"

The question was answered with silence, save for the crashing waves and the belabored grunts of hunters tripping in the sand and spilling all of their water. Brían looked up for the first time, his wings furled against his body, guilt seeming to glitter in his eyes as he kept his gaze on Camaráin. The boy reached out, hoping to find something, *feel* something, that would indicate even the slightest Bond. But there was nothing.

The selkie rose her hand, warmth exuding from her long fingers. "It would seem I owe you all an explanation. But you most of all, young one." The heat dissipated from her hand as she looked at Camaráin, trailing away in wisps and surrounding him, the closest to a Bond he had yet felt, but vanishing in the same instance.

Nil rose to her feet, walking away from the group and resting a hand against a nearby tree. "The history of the land of Nóra is one often intertwined with both the dragons and the fae, though the histories of man would seek to deny it. The dragons blessed this land with beauty and wealth and good health, while we fae were tasked with the well-being of Nóra's people. The hearts of man are kept well because we desired it to be so. It was our inclination to create a union of our blessings, to bridge the blessings of the dragons to the blessings of the fae, to forge a bridge from the hearts of man to the hearts of the land. It is thanks to we fae that the Bond between dragons and humans exists."

"I beg your pardon?" Áine stood, her eyes wide. "That cannot be—surely there would be some record of it!"

"You expect much of the willingness of man to record that which he does not understand." A smile stretched across Nil's face. "I ask you, how precisely do you believe dragons and humans came to Bond with one another?"

Áine's head lowered, a frustrated grunt escaping her lips.

"I...I didn't believe there to be an explanation. There simply *was*."

Shaking her head, Nil said, "Nothing comes to be for no reason. All that is and all that will be is the result of something else."

"So there's a 'reason' why you have taken the Bond with Brían for yourself?" Camaráin said with a snarl. His lips quivered, his eyes fluttering as he tried not to let his angry tears fall. Tried, and failed, for his tears had already been falling for some time.

"Camaráin, please," Granma said, extending a hand toward her grandson. "She has taken nothing."

Nil sunk her head and raised a hand. "It is alright. I understand his frustration. The Bond was rightfully a moment of excitement for both dragon and man before the Inquisition, but that is regrettably no more." She crossed her arms over her chest, walking slowly toward the group. "Beyond our intertwined histories, we fae have long felt a measure of camaraderie with the dragons, but especially so since the days of the Inquisition and the dragons' exile beyond the Cliffs of Ard. We share in one another's pain at now being 'unwanted' in Nóra, though we never did determine the reason we have received the Priory's ire. It seems to change every generation or so. I believe the current reason is the High Prior split his trousers during a sermon and could not find a tailor to blame. I suppose it is easier to blame an invisible faerie than it is to admit you have grown fat.

"But our scattering across Nóra held similar impact to the land as did the dragons' exile. The blessings bequeathed by the dragons began to fade, and the land grew less vibrant and verdant, the sun refusing to shine with the same frequency. For us, the hearts of man grew angrier, more violent in our absence, which meant the gnomes felt right at home, but the rest of us wished to remain far away.

"And it also had a larger consequence: the dwindling numbers of the Bonded Ones. The dragons may have been exiled, but those with whom they Bonded vanished, either jailed, or exiled, or forced to work in the food service industry. I suppose some remained hidden enough to establish the order of the Draconic Priests, but those Bonded abilities do not pass through hereditary means, do they?" Nil directed the question at Granma.

Granma pointed a finger at Áine. "I think you mean her. I'm not that old."

Áine shook her head, regardless.

A solemn expression took over Nil's face as she looked at Brían. "Neither we nor the dragons wished for the Bonded Ones to fade to the secret histories of the Draconic Priests. We had given up hope of there ever being another human to be counted among the ranks of the Bonded...and so we made an agreement."

Camaráin's ears perked at the mention of an "agreement." His heart sank just the same.

"An agreement to Bond dragon to fae," Nil continued. "Each generation, an egg would be presented to us in secret, though it had never been anything more than a ceremonial gesture. Never had there been a *need* to Bond with one another, per se. It was simply because..." She trailed off, a frown on her lips as she glanced at Camaráin. "Because we never expected this day would ever come, where man and dragon would be once again Bonded. We did not want the world to move on without the beauty of the Bond.

"And I was the one chosen for such a Bond this time. Thank the heavens for that, too, because it was between me and a gnome. I am unsure what happened to him, but I heard he escaped a hunt and may be elsewhere in the capital region now."

Camaráin looked to Ma and Granma, who returned the same suspicious exchanges. If it was the same gnome they were thinking of...it still remained a mystery why the couch exploded.

Nil did not notice the silent conversation and continued with her own. "Tinaeron's parents had long since passed from this world, and without them, it was doubtful the egg would hatch on its own. Even after I Bonded with him, I could hardly have imagined the adventure he was to take after being re-turned to the Highlands, though." Slowly, she looked at Ca-maráin, and offered an appreciative nod. "You have my grati-tude for keeping him safe, young one."

Gnawing at his lower lip, Camaráin's hands continued to shake as he still tried to quell his anger toward the selkie.

"I know that you are frustrated," she said. "I know that you do not believe you were keeping him safe for me. But know that I now have a large responsibility with being the only Bonded One among the fae. These hunters, these..." She stopped to roll her eyes. "...Fae Smashers, they have been targeting us for long enough. But now, we finally have the chance to defend ourselves. *I* have that chance."

Brían unfurled his wings and looked at Nil with a demon-strable measure of pride, but he still flashed a glance at Camaráin, hesitation evident.

That was not lost on the boy. He took a step forward, holding his shaking hands in place, and said, "I know that, and I understand. But even if he and I aren't connected like you are, even if he and I won't share that same connection that my sister has with her dragon, Brían and I still have a bond of our own! We've read together, we've shared a bed together, we've adventured together. I kept him safe from a smuggler and brigands and our governor and the Inquisition! We're still bonded just the same!"

Ma grasped Camaráin's shoulders, pressing down. "It's okay, Cam. Just calm down."

Nil raised a finger. "Back up a second. Your sister is a Bonded One, too?"

His mouth agape, Camaráin outturned his hands and shrugged his shoulders. He opened his mouth to say more, but Nil rose a second finger.

"Second point, let us quiet down. We have company."

Walking toward the woods was the head of the Fac Smashers himself, only slightly on fire.

Chapter Twenty-One

The intimidation exuded by Robeárd, smoke wafting off his black leathers against the backdrop of the blazes behind him, was undercut by the clumsy panic of his men trying to douse the fire in desperation. He could have been the embodiment of fear, the champion of death itself, and it would still do little frighten Camaráin while he watched two men spilling seawater all over themselves and tripping over themselves in a mud pile of their own making.

Camaráin huddled close to his ma and granma, Áine standing watch behind them. Una remained undeterred, her face showing not fear or panic, but disdain for the man approaching them. Nil waved her hand at her waist, almost imperceptible had Camaráin not been looking in her direction, and at the motion, the surrounding faeries dispersed, and with them their illumination.

Though he knew he no longer had cause to fear the Inquisition—regardless of the fact that Robeárd was not an Inquisitor—Camaráin still opened the top of his pack and flexed his shoulder, demanding on instinct that Brían hide himself away in the canvas. The dragon's absence still weighed heavily on him, despite the hatchling being a short distance away at Nil's feet.

The leader of the Fae Smashers reached the edge of the forest and stopped, his hands on his hips in a show of authority, though one of those exaggerated displays, like he was imitating the statue of Cormac the Uniter, a great king from the days of antiquity who united the clans of Nóra under one banner nine hundred years ago, though Robeárd was coming across more as the statue of Fingus the Ruiner, who dissolved that union eight hundred and ninety-nine years ago by starting a war because he never checked his mail for the memo. Why there were statues of both men in Mór, Camaráin did not know, not that they got the opportunity to visit the monuments, but it still seemed silly to him to go through the trouble of memorializing the losing side.

Regardless, Fingus Reborn stood before them, his sneer cold but his posture anything but natural. There was a tension in the woods as the chittering of the faeries fell silent. There was near enough an aura of hatred wafting off of Nil, for all Camaráin could tell. They stood in the woods, exchanging not a single word between them, all the while Robeárd peered into the woods with the same silent regard. Camaráin held his breath, hoping that if they maintained this silence for long enough, the man would walk away.

After a long, quiet moment, the hunter finally said, "Do you need help, or what?"

"Oh, he can see us." Camaráin kicked at a rock with disappointment.

"I have hunter's eyes," Robeárd added. "It is quite useful when finding my quarry at night."

Áine pointed at him. "Your hunter's eyes missed the fire on

your shoulder."

Robeárd nodded. "They did. But a man backs away from no pain."

"It's scorching your cloak."

"You're right. Please excuse me." The Fae Smasher flung the cloak off his shoulders and stamped it into the sand to extinguish it, working his boot through sharp and pained breaths.

Leaning in close, Una said, "Looks like that's the closest he'll come to smashing anything."

No one laughed, but it was worth commending her for effectively using sarcasm for the first time. Áine shook the scholar's hand.

The fire quelled, his cloak in cinders, and his shoulder smoldering, Robeárd turned back on his heel and reassumed his prior position, gritting his teeth in clear pain, though it was clear he was trying not to show it (he failed). "I could not help but notice you all from afar. It seems you have lost your way. These words are unsafe. I would bring you back to the sanctity of Mór, if you would permit it."

"How chivalrous of you," Ma said, with little humor in her voice. "And here I thought knights in shining armor were only on the mainland."

"It is not for me to know what the mainland dwellers do. However, it is clear that I am not wearing shining armor at all."

Right. The whole "no sarcasm" thing. Though he couldn't see her—mostly because he didn't have eyes in the back of his head like his ma did—Camaráin could *feel* Áine rolling her eyes.

Discarding the exaggerated power stance, Robeárd made to bow before the women and child, saying, "But if you'll permit me, I'll be happy to guide you back to—wait a moment, I know you." His eyes traveled beyond Camaráin and his family, narrowing toward Una. "I believe I've seen you at sermons. Luna, isn't it?"

"Una," she corrected.

"That's what I said."

"No, it isn't."

Robeárd hummed a raspy note in his throat. He remained a half-bow, but somehow managed to put his hands back on his hips and look more threatening. "Just why *are* you in these fae woods, Tuna?"

"It's Una."

"No, it's not."

Una rolled her eyes, muttering something under her breath. Ma cupped her hands over Camaráin's ears while Una was mid-word, so he didn't catch it. He wondered if she was speaking something in the gnomish tongue.

Taking a step forward, the researcher huffed a sigh and said, "These are some friends from out of town. I thought to take them down to the shore to watch the sunset, and we lost track of time after that."

Robeárd furrowed his brow, standing tall once more, reverting to his nonthreatening appearance. "Have you not heard the High Prior's warnings? The fae wander these shores. It is not safe for such a young woman to be venturing, especially at night."

"What about strength in numbers?" Una shrugged her shoulders. "I think we will get by just fine."

His eyes traveling from person to person, Robeárd frowned and shook his head. "I would be remiss in my duties to leave five women and a child alone in these woods. I don't think your cat will be much help either."

Camaráin raised an eyebrow in confusion and eyed Brían. The dragon looked just as confused. He mewled in an approximation of a cat's meow, which was shockingly accurate. He had never even encountered a cat before.

"Therefore," Robeárd continued, but his gaze lingered on Nil.

Among the group, glances passed between one another, silently asking if they should act before Nil's identity was discovered. Or, at least, that was what Camaráin was thinking. The women seemed to be debating something else entirely, though Camaráin was left in the dark on that one.

"You there!" Robeárd finally said, pointing at Nil. Tension gripped the air as his voice echoed in the woods, while one of his comrades was screaming in the distance as though he were on fire. As a blur of fire ran toward the ocean, the head of the Fae Smashers said, "Are you unwell? Your skin has taken on a foul color."

Camaráin turned his head to look at Nil. Even in her disguised form, the selkie had retained her sea-green skin color.

Nil remained calm. She nodded and said, "Thank you, but I am well. I'm just...from the north."

The hunter grunted his assent, nodding.

The wind whipped with the speed Áine turned her head toward Ma. She began to mouth something but Ma covered Camaráin's eyes while she was midway through. He'd never learn gnomish at this rate.

"At any rate," Robeárd said, "I must reiterate how unsafe this area is. I will offer once more to escort you back to Mór after my duties are concluded tonight."

Una quickly shook her head. "We'll pass. We feel perfectly safe."

"If the threat of the fae will not deter you, do you not see the *inferno* threatening to engulf the city?" he said, pointing at the wall of flame.

"It wouldn't be the first time this has happened."

"Nor the second."

"Nor the fourth."

"Our people have a sordid history with starting fires directly south of the city, don't we?"

"On that, we agree."

Beyond Robeárd, one of the hunters took to bellowing a war cry and charging at the fire with a helmet filled with sand. Somehow, it would all work out, probably.

"We do thank you for your offered kindness," Nil said in her melodic voice, breaking up the reminiscing of pyromaniacal days. "But it should be noted that these shores seemed quite safe before the fire broke out."

The hunter grumbled, rolling his eyes, and said, "Fine. If you wish to risk your lives, then so be it. Just tell me this: have any of you seen a selkie?"

"No."

"Uh-uh."

"I have not."

"Regrettably, no."

"Ugh."

Head shaking.

"Meow."

With a huff, Robeárd shook his head and turned on his heel.

"A waste of time," he muttered. "All this time could have been spent finding and taming that weird horse." He began to walk away.

"Wait," Una said, stepping forward. "Did you say a 'horse?'"

Robeárd stopped, turning over his shoulder. "What of it, Kuna?"

"It's Una."

"It's unimportant. What *of* it?"

Stifling a chuckle, Nil fashioned an amused smile and said, "I believe you're thinking of a kelpie. *They* more resemble horses. I've not heard anything about them coming to the shores of Nóra, however."

Freezing in place, the hunter turned to fully face Nil. Disbelief colored his face. It could have been for a number of reasons: why someone would know of the difference between a selkie and a kelpie, why they would know a kelpie was not often found in Nóra, or why she seemed amused by the mix-up to begin with. But instead, Robeárd craned his head to the sky and bellowed in frustration. "*WHY DID THEY NOT TELL ME THAT?*" he screamed.

"A little confusion as to what you're hunting?" Una said, masking her own pleasure at the sight. She couldn't seem to stop the corner of her lip from creasing upward.

"You *idiots*!" Robeárd faced the wall of flame once again and sprinted toward it, shaking his fist all the way. "*Why did you not correct me?! We've wasted so much time!*" His voice faded over the horizon against the crackling of flames and the shouts of his men to put out said flames.

The crisis was averted for now, at least. A collective sigh of relief was released as they all sat in a circle. Camaráin's hands were no longer shaking, and instead, all he could do was watch Robeárd leave, his anger redirected toward his men who seemed a bit too preoccupied to address his ire.

"And this is who the Priory is trying to use to ignite another Inquisition," Áine said.

"They fit the bill," Ma added. "The last one was started by man's stupidity."

"There has to be something we can do," Camaráin murmured, his voice carrying further than he thought. The idle conversations quieted, and they all looked in his direction. "Right?"

Though he intended for the question to hang listlessly in the air, it drifted its way toward the selkie. A smile remained on Nil's face, but the warmth of it had vanished. "There is nothing further that requires your assistance, young one. You have done more than enough." Her long fingers found their way along Brían's neck, caressing the dragon's scales. "This is but the lot of the fae. We may stop these hunters today, but they will always return in some form or another. At least now, we have the means to defend ourselves." She smiled at Brían, who responded with another meow, even though he didn't need to pretend to be a cat anymore.

"But you're just one person," Camaráin said. "Selkie. Fae. Ma'am. You can't be everywhere."

Nil nodded. "I can't be everywhere," she agreed. "But I can be somewhere. We are a resourceful people, so you need not worry. Wherever I may not be, we will endure. The pixies and faeries hide well in these woods. We sea-dwellers can retreat underwater for as long as need be. The gnomes will do as the gnomes do, whether it is creating shelter among the trees or hiding in the caves beneath the bluffs over there—" She pointed across the shoreline, where the land stood tall above the sea. "—but as much as your concern is appreciated, there is simply no need to—"

"No." Camaráin looked at the selkie, then silently voiced an apology to Ma for rudely interrupting. He glanced toward Robeárd and his hunters, hands bunching once more into fists. "I'm not going to accept that, and neither should you. At least now while *he's* still around."

"Cam?" Ma said.

The selkie tilted her head, her curiosity evidently piqued. "What do you propose?"

Camaráin looked to the sea, and the bluffs beyond. Perhaps a taste of the hunter's own medicine was in store. "I have an idea."

Nil lifted a hand, the heat from her Bond with Brían radiating. "Do you propose I be more...accurate this time?"

"What?" Camaráin raised an eyebrow and shook his head. "No. Not at all."

She quelled her flames. "Spoilsport."

Chapter Twenty-Two

"Come now, pick up the pace! Have you never put out a fire before?"

"Heavens above, man, no! Do we look like a fire brigade?"

"Normally we *start* the fires, sir! All's best to draw 'em out, you always say!"

"Right, but that's how we burned down the original cathedral!"

"That was overblown. It were only the façade what burned!"

"It did run into conflict with our motto, though: 'No property damage.'"

"Old name, old motto!"

"What's the new motto, then?"

"'No, property damage!'"

Dousing the fire was getting nowhere. Luckily, it hadn't spread too far to the north, and the sea breeze was gentle, but Robeárd knew it would reflect poorly on him if the Fae Smashers lived up to their new slogan. This time, it wasn't his fault, though.

All he could do was shake his head. His two volunteer firefighters had lost their battle against the fire. One was presently going for a swim, and the other took to playing volleyball with those on the other side of the flames. Where he even found a volleyball was beyond Robeárd's ken—it wasn't even a sport in Nóra.

Above all, though, he was in the throes of disappointment. Largely at his men for neglecting to inform him that he was hunting the *wrong* creature all this time. He had no idea what a selkie even was. For all he knew, he could have been talking to one this whole time and didn't know it. But that'd be ridiculous. It would surely be obvious.

His shoulder still hurt from where it had caught fire. Not his brightest idea, but he did see that group in the woods—what else was he to do, let the fae take them? He'd learned his lesson, though: no more jumping through fire. He wished he was on the other side of it, though. All of his stuff was over there. He sighed. "Of all the nights for it *not* to rain."

Taking a seat, Robeárd stared at the woods, no longer seeing that strange group within. He rolled his eyes at their idiocy. They were entreating their own funeral, so far as he was concerned. Especially with how the trees were rustling. And how much noise they were making. Why the trees sounded like a horse was not for him to know. Just more fae nonsense, surely.

Leaning back and closing his eyes, Robeárd thought it a good idea to rest with the flames keeping him warm. Then he realized that was a dumb idea, just in time for a volleyball to get spiked into his knee.

As his eyes bulged open, the trees seemed to part. Or, perhaps it was more accurate to say that the trees themselves were emerging from the woods. The wind took on a life of its own as a form burst forth, green as the trees themselves. It landed with a heavy thud, the flames growing taller, much to the chagrin of his men, whose volleyball game just became more difficult. Robeárd shielded his eyes against the fire, but as he lowered his arm, he took in the sight of the creature who had just emerged: a horse of sea-green coloring, its mane dripping wet as though it just swam in the ocean. Its eyes glimmered with an icy-blue light, almost coming across as a threat.

Robeárd rose to his feet, his heart thumping in his chest. He reached for his tools, forgetting they were on the other side of the wall of fire. He'd just have to get creative, then. Pointing at the creature, he drew in a breath and shouted, "Kelpie!"

"Oh, *now* you know what a kelpie is, do you?" said the hunter nearest to him.

"Never mind that! Form up! The hunt is on!"

"But it's match point, sir!" shouted one of the hunters on the other side of the flames.

The kelpie snorted and dug its front hoof into the sand, readying to charge. Before Robeárd could blink, the creature lurched forward, directly toward him, armless though he was...but it turned at the last moment, galloping in the direction of the bluffs overlooking the sea.

"Oh, forget you all!" Robeárd spat. "You bring shame to the Fae Smasher name!" He ran after the kelpie without a plan, nothing except he would bring it to heel with his bare hands if he had to.

As he left the sand and battled through the tangles of thorns and vines in pursuit of the beast, he could have sworn he heard someone say, "The name 'Fae Smasher' brings shame to the Fae Smasher name."

Thorns scraped and clawed against his leathers, but he didn't care. He had a task, and he would see it done. The kelpie did not seem to be galloping at full speed, either. He wondered if it was injured, or if it was merely challenging him. Either way, all the better for him.

As he cleared the thorns, Robeárd found his second wind, sprinting after the kelpie with an energy he no longer knew he had. He had captured numerous fae over the years under the employ of the Priory, but it had almost always been faeries and pixies. But *this*...this was a challenge he liked. This was a challenge he had dreamed of, ever since that time he had dreamed of this specific challenge. He couldn't say why it was; he was just wired that way. Some men wish to become great scholars, and others want to hunt creatures of the fae for sport. Someone had to do it.

The kelpie continued to gallop at a slow pace as though to goad him on. "Your overconfidence will be your undoing!" Robeárd yelled at it, reaching out a hand but failing to grasp its tail. Granted, the tail was still several yards away, but it never hurt to try.

After a third wind hit him, he snarled and dove for the horse, but missed, his hand just grazing the edge of its hoof, his fingers coming away damp. The kelpie trotted around him, snorting as though with derision, and leaped over his prone form. If ever there was a moment for it to trample him, it was then, but it only taunted him. He wouldn't stand for that, even as he was lying down.

Pushing himself back to his feet, Robeárd growled and followed the kelpie's path, its mocking face whinnying in challenge. He rolled his shoulder, ignoring the discomfort radiating from the burns, and sprinted after it, drawing closer, closer, closer, near enough to touch, his hand gliding across its tail, a few strands of hair catching between his fingers. All he needed was to close the gap. Three more steps, two more, one. He lurched forward once more, the kelpie just now within his grasp.

And his feet left him. The kelpie continued to move forward, but he was going down. A pit opened in his stomach, and when he looked down, only the sea was there to greet him. The saltwater stung against his shoulder, but it was a mercy that the water was deep enough that he was not hurt otherwise.

When he breached, the kelpie had vanished. His first instinct was to swim forward, but rock formations stood tall before him. He looked at his surroundings and considered himself all too lucky that he landed in the water and not on the rocks. If only there was an easy way to climb out of here; the rocks were much too high.

Luckily, there was a cave nearby. If nothing else, he could wait out the night, get his bearings come the break of dawn, and start this hunt all over again. Slapping the face of the water in frustration, he gritted his teeth and swam to the cave beneath the bluffs, happy to at least have this spot for respite.

Dry land felt wonderful, even if his soaked clothes did not. He sat at the mouth of the cave, huddling together for warmth, and grumbled to himself, "'Kelpies don't come to Nóra,' my foot. Shows what you know, lady." He scoffed. "Northerners."

He closed his eyes, hoping for a few moments of relaxation.

He was granted exactly one moment before he heard a round of murmuring behind him. His eyes shot open and he rose to his knees, turning around to see four small men with long white beards approaching. Black and beady eyes were just barely visible from underneath their red knit caps. It was only when their murmurings became angrier and more nonsensical that Robeárd realized his error.

Jumping to his feet, he spread his hands wide open to show that he had nothing with which to harm them. "Lads, please. How about we talk this over?"

There was no talking when gnomes were involved—largely because few could actually speak the same tongue as the gnomes. At the front of the pack, the lead gnome showed a row of large teeth and began to crack his knuckles. Another grabbed a nearby chair and broke it on the ground. The third was flexing his jaw, and the fourth was already kicking Robeárd in the shins.

The hunter groaned. It was going to be a long night, indeed.

Chapter Twenty-Three

The fires went out on their own, eventually. So far as the hunters were concerned, at the very least. One moment they were playing volleyball, and the next, the wall of flame vanished entirely, leaving little evidence except for the charred grass, smoldering bushes, stench of burning, and a few wounds that probably should have been looked at by an apothecary a while ago. The remaining hunters picked up their things and left just as quickly, sopping wet or scorched dry, grumbling all the while that they hated this job the whole time and that maybe it was time to give being a barber another shot.

Camaráin stood at the edge of the woods with a smug feeling of satisfaction. He leaned against a tree with his arms crossed, watching the Fae Smashers depart with no attention heeded to either him or his family and friends. Ma and Áine wrapped their arms around his shoulders, Una scribbling a note down of the evening's proceedings, and Granma huffed a deep breath.

"The next time I need to get rid of a gnome, I think I'll just call an exterminator," she said, dark bags pooling under her eyes.

And nestling at Camaráin's feet was the familiar warmth of the dragon he had held and protected as an egg, shared in knowledge and joy after his hatching, and ultimately lost due to circumstances beyond the control of either of them. Brían flexed his wings and sat calmly next to Camaráin, a contented trill rumbling in his throat.

How much longer he had to share in the dragon's company, he could not say, but Camaráin was grateful that he had this much time to begin with. Though the lack of a Bond prevented him from having any way of knowing, he liked to think Brían felt the same. Or was at least approaching the same. It was hard to tell with him most of the time.

The waves calmed to silence, only to burst in another torrent as Nil emerged from beneath the sea, first in her natural selkie form, and then just as quickly to her human form so she could walk on land. Camaráin's heart remained heavy at the sight of her, especially as Brían unfurled his wings with her return, but the anger was beginning to quell, even if the sadness would not.

The selkie approached, seawater dripping from her hair as it clung to her skin. Though her presence spoke to the group at large, her attention was placed squarely on Camaráin. She put her hand to her chest in a show of gratitude and offered a slight bow, a smile refusing to leave her face. "You have my thanks, young one."

Camaráin shrugged the compliment aside. "You did all the hard work. If you can change form at will, why haven't you done that before?"

Ma swatted him on the shoulder.

Nil chuckled. "The simple answer? It is difficult." She extended her hands outward as she shrugged. "And were we shapeshifters all to take the forms of one another, it would simply grow too complicated and confusing for all parties involved."

"That's a good point," Camaráin said with a nod. "One time, my sister and I swapped clothes, and Ma couldn't tell us apart for two weeks."

"I was humoring you both, Cam," Ma said in response. "Adults aren't as foolish as you take them to be."

"The Inquisition was."

"They were the exception."

"What about the Fae Smashers?"

"Uneducated and led by a fool but could turn it around with the right person in charge."

Nil cleared her throat. "If I may?" She inclined her head, awaiting further discussion of the folly and stupidity of man, but nothing followed. With a smile, she said to Camaráin, "You are quite clever for one your age. I must commend you for that."

"Oh, we had dragons throw the bad guys into the sea on our last adventure, so I can't take all the credit." Camaráin flashed his teeth at Áine.

"Don't look at me," Áine said. "I'm not stealing credit from the dragons."

"What about those gnomes, though?" Ma asked. "Should we not be concerned that Robeárd is...well, you know." She ran a finger across her exposed neck.

Una laughed but was quick to shake her head. "Oh, no. Gnomes would never do that. The worst they will do to a person is destroy their self-confidence. Gnomes may be angry, but they're also selective toward whom they throw their anger. Robeárd could very well be curling up into a ball and sucking his thumb for the rest of his days."

Áine smiled and laughed at the notion.

"What's funny? I'm quite serious."

"Oh, come on. You had *just* learned sarcasm, too."

"Am I now to *only* speak with sarcasm? I don't understand."

"Lord above, the sooner I can return to the north, the better."

"Are the woods more exciting than the city?"

"They're much less backwards, at least!"

The conversation between Áine and Una devolved into jabs thrown at one another's preferred places of dwelling, while Ma and Granma walked off on their own seemingly to discuss literally anything else (Camaráin heard mention of "antiquing" and "never setting foot inside Mór again," but it was hard to parse out the conversation from that little).

Which left Nil alone with the boy and the dragon. A story Camaráin had promised his ma would be different from the last time, but he could hardly have imagined just how different it would be from a few short weeks ago. Part of him wished he and Ma had not accepted Granma and Granda's invitation and let them sort out the business with Cousin Gnome all on their own. Granda seemed to have solved it without their help anyway. But he felt he would have been happier had he not learned of his fate with Brían—or that fate would not intertwine them at all. If all he could have done was stay in his room and read books with his dragon, that would have been enough.

But he knew that wasn't the story for him. For either of them. And just as the story begins, so, too, must it end.

Camaráin straightened himself out as Nil drew nearer, Brían trilling at his feet, a medley of emotions audible in the noise—happiness, sadness, distress, frustration, maybe a little bit of hunger. Always difficult to get a read on, that one.

The selkie folded her hands at her waist, her eyes flitting between Camaráin and Brían, the smile on her face losing its enthusiasm, overtaken instead by a show of grief to match the boy's. "For what it is worth, young one, I am sorry that my Bond with Tinaeron prevented one of your own. Would that I had known the Bonded Ones were soon to return."

Shaking his head, Camaráin chewed the inside of his lip and said, "You couldn't have known. I didn't think any of this was possible until a month ago. My sister is still the only one. It'll still be a long time before it's all back to normal again."

Nil chuckled at that, her eyes downcast. "Yesterday's normal is today's strange, and vice versa. Worry not about making today the same as yesterday and focus instead on making tomorrow better than today. I believe...we fae can look to a better tomorrow with thanks to you today."

"That tomorrow involves *him*, though, doesn't it?" Camaráin kneeled beside Brían, the dragon glancing at him with hesitation. Flashes of the first few days after his hatching showed in his face, where he was all too eager to remain at the boy's side. Before the pull of the fae dragged him further from Camaráin.

With hand outstretched, Camaráin managed a smile at the hatchling, even as tears threatened to break. And Brían, for his part...rested his chin right in the boy's palm. The warmth of his ruby-red scales was all the parting he needed. Any more would only have made it worse.

Camaráin slowly pulled his hand away, the dragon unprepared for his face to fall into the sand. Voicing a quick apology, Camaráin ran his hand down Brían's neck one more time and backed away, letting there be space for the dragon to go off to his next journey without him hovering over him.

Nil crouched to one knee and offered her long hand to the dragon, beckoning him forward just as Camaráin did. The boy knew he owed it to Brían to see him off, even if this is where he was always meant to be, no matter how much it hurt to see Brían take that first step toward the selkie. No matter how much it stung to watch Brían stop midway through the second step to look back at him.

And no matter how much it confused him to watch Brían turn around and walk back to him.

And all the more, no matter how much it relieved him to see Nil react not with anger or spite at being spurned in such a way...but with joy.

Brían took his time slithering against the small dunes of the shore—barely a step for Camaráin, but an annoying navigation for a young dragon—and stopped just shy of Camaráin, his face showing a hesitant approximated smile, but the glint in his eyes speaking louder than any words.

Home.

The selkie rose back to her feet, dusting the sand off her knee. "The one thing I detest about walking on dry land. I never liked sand. So rough and...irritating." Reorienting herself, she flung away the specks of sand from her palm and eyed the pair once more. "Young one. No, *Camaráin*. There will come times where I will have need of Tinaeron—that, I cannot deny. But...so long as you can accept that, I believe the dragon has made his choice."

The sinking pit in his stomach vanished, his breath caught in the back of his throat, and the tears may as well have been sucked right back into his eyes. Camaráin could do nothing but leave his mouth agape, bereft of the words to say. He heard the group filing in behind him against the backdrop of gasps and sharp whispers, but all he could muster for himself was a stammered, "N-Nil? Are...are you...?"

Nodding, the selkie walked toward Camaráin and placed a hand on his shoulder, while caressing the back of Brían's head with her other hand. "If ever I am to need him, he will know, for our Bond is strong already...but so, too, is the bond he has forged with you." She winked at Brían. "Even if he is loath to admit it sometimes."

Brían's breath caught, and he turned his head as though it was some great secret divulged.

Whether secret or not, Camaráin could not help himself from pulling the dragon tight in his arms, drawing a gasp and a frantic fluttering of wings, but no resistance otherwise. No words were necessary—Bond or not, Camaráin knew that this was where the dragon, *his* dragon, was happiest.

The adults circled around him, taking in the scene with joyful overlapping conversations. Áinc spoke of one thing or another about her draconic research, Una remarked that she had no idea Áine was a researcher, insults about Mór were exchanged, and Ma and Granma wrapped themselves around Camaráin, joining him in his happiness.

The dragon broke free of Camaráin's grasp and coughed on the ground, though this time, he did not hide his mirth. He seemed eager to jump right back into the boy's arms.

"As long as you're okay that I won't be able to draw on the Bond, you're welcome with us as long as you want, Brían," Camaráin whispered to the dragon as he continued to hold him near.

"FINE BY ME!" Ma shouted, her voice rife with anxiety.

They all laughed, Nil included. The selkie turned her attention back to the sea. Back home. Already her body was beginning to illuminate, seemingly eager to return to her natural appearance.

"What will you do now?" Una asked.

With a noncommittal grunt, Nil said, "Who's to say? There are still some hunters lurking about, I'm sure. But I can always trick a few of them and dwindle them down that way." She winked.

The women chuckled, but Camaráin remained confused. "I don't get it."

"Don't worry about it," Ma said.

"And what of you all?" Nil asked the group. "Will you stay in Mór?"

"Heavens, no," Áine responded without a second thought.

"Back home for us," Ma said, gripping Camaráin by the shoulder.

"I need to make sure my house is still standing," Granma added, woe in her voice.

"*Heh*, very good," Nil said. She nodded a quick goodbye to Una, and turned back toward the sea, her legs beginning to take their natural form once more.

As the selkie reached the shoreline, Granma's comment hung in Camaráin's head, and he ran after her. "Nil, wait!"

The selkie turned her head over her shoulder, wordlessly awaiting his question.

"What do we do if a gnome decides to move into our house? Hypothetically."

All Nil could do was chuckle. "Pray for the best of luck." And she dove back into the sea.

Epilogue

They returned to Mór as dawn broke. It was one of the rare days when the sun decided to make an appearance, which, according to legend, meant that somewhere, a dragon was happy.

Well, it wasn't actually according to legend. Camaráin just decided it was because he knew Brían was happy, and he had very little else to go on to suggest otherwise.

Regardless, Camaráin felt an extra spring in his step that had been missing for quite some time, and it was reciprocated by the dragon. Brían sat happily atop the boy's shoulders, a contented sigh escaping his mouth more than once.

The same could be said for the adults. Where the walk to the shoreline had been one conducted in morose silence, the return to the city was filled with mirthful conversation and copious laughter. Not once did Áine and Una discuss the absurdity of Mór, which one could say was a big plus.

Even the citizens of Mór reflected that same cheerfulness. Dawn had only broken less than an hour ago, but they all took to the streets in droves, exchanging pleasantries and even remaining nonplussed by the tourists pointing at the sun while staring directly into it.

Camaráin could not help but feel even more overwhelmed by the number of people than he was before, but that couldn't be stopped. No one even seemed to recognize there was a massive fire just to the south. This city truly was strange.

The group wandered around for a bit, in no rush despite it being clear Granma was worrying for the state of the house after being away for so long. Camaráin assured her nothing bad would happen in a story like this, to which she responded with confusion and questions of what the devil he was even talking about.

Their aimless wandering eventually brought them to the small and quiet square where Brían had been chased a faerie. Back before Robeárd made his presence known. Back before this adventure seemed to start in earnest. So much had changed, and everything that had seemed was for the worse actually ended up for the better.

"Well," Una said as they sat on the bench in the grass, "I think this is where we part ways for now. The others are probably worried sick for me."

"You think so?" Camaráin asked.

She shrugged. "I don't know. I forget about them sometimes." She rose to her feet, dusting off the remnants of sand from her trousers. "It's certainly been quite the experience. Thanks for helping Nil out. It couldn't have been done without you."

"Again, she did most of the work."

"Most of the work that would have been impossible without you. Well, without the dragon, anyway. Sorry about all that, by the by."

"Don't ever do it again," Áine warned, crossing her arms.

With a slow nod, Una responded, "I'll keep that in mind for the next time a selkie asks me to find their dragon." She chuckled, staring down an alleyway in the vague direction of where her fellows' hidden library was, probably. "I can't say it didn't make for good research, though."

Áine opened her mouth to rebuke her, but Ma jumped in before she got the chance. "Don't say a word, Áine. You were mentally taking down notes just the same."

"Fine, fine." Áine smirked and extended her hand toward Una. "Take care of yourself. Hopefully your scholarship won't remain forbidden for much longer."

Una took her hand and shook it in kind. "I'm sure you'd know a thing or two about that." She stood in silence for a moment, contemplation evident on her face, a couple quick laughs thrown in. She neglected to share in the humor, though. It was probably Mór humor, though, so there likely wasn't much to laugh at. "I'm sure it won't take long," she finally said. "These things always have a way of figuring themselves out sooner rather than later."

"If you say so."

"But," she added, "if ever I'm in need of more Fae Smasher Smashers, I'll come find you."

"Is this the name we're going to settle on?" Ma asked.

They all laughed, and no one offered a better name. Una said goodbye to them all individually, save for a scratch for Brían on the back of his head, and disappeared into the nearest alleyway, her shadow vanishing in an instant.

"Do you think she ever gets lost in those alleys?" Camaráin asked.

Áine chuckled. "Oh, I hope so."

After a few minutes more, they returned to the city's main thoroughfare, just in time to pass the cathedral and have their eardrums ruptured by its bell. For a moment, Camaráin felt he could see through time for how dizzy the explosion of noise made him.

When they all returned to consciousness, they noticed the High Prior giving a sermon on the front steps of the cathedral. Camaráin hadn't known what to expect the man to look like, and even this close, he still couldn't tell. Almost all of his body was covered in gaudy and garish robes, and his hat had sunken so low that only his mouth remained uncovered. He still moved above with the confidence of a man who could see where he was going, so at least he had that going for him.

There was a small congregation, much fewer than to be expected with a cathedral this size. Sermons typically included a lot of kneeling, and given there were no pews to indicate where to kneel outside, it seemed most got confused and went to do other things that were less confusing.

"And, so, I say unto ye!" the High Prior shouted at the apex of his sermon. "Why is it that selkies and kelpies shall bear a name so similar? They are inviting only confusion into our daily lives!"

He was instantly met with boos. At a glance, Camaráin could spot a few of the Fae Smashers in the crowd. Somewhere, they had found tomatoes—strange, given they were not native to Nóra—and began to throw them at the High Prior.

If this was how mass typically went, Camaráin would have been inclined to go more often.

"Alright, then," Granma said, pushing the boy along. "Shall we be off?" From the force of her nudging, it was clearly not a genuine inquiry.

Beag stood as it always did—quiet, quaint, and smelling of the elderly. Nothing had changed at all in the time they were in and around the capital.

Including, much to Granma's great relief, her house.

No evidence of damage, miraculous reconstruction, or other general tomfoolery, major or minor. But as they drew nearer, the commotion within the house froze Granma in her tracks, her hand hovering over the doorknob.

Ma patted her on the back with a smile. "Shall we get this over with?" she asked.

Granma let loose a long and wavering breath, turned the knob, pushed the door open...

And found the interior absolutely immaculate. The floor had been cleaned, the houseplants repotted, the furniture reupholstered, the walls repainted, and somehow there was another story on the house. It didn't look that way from the outside.

Camaráin smirked as he watched Granma stammer with confusion, befuddled further by the sight of Granda and Cousin Gnome singing in the kitchen, clinking together two large mugs, arms wrapped around one another's shoulders.

"AND THERE'S A HAND, MY TRUSTY FEIRE, AND GIE'S A HAND O' THINE!" Granda and the gnome belted at the top of their lungs.

Granma cleared her throat. "Padraig?"

"AND WE'LL TAK A RIGHT GUDE-WILLIE WAUGHT, FOR AULD LANG SYNE!"

"*PADRAIG!*"

Granda startled, nearly spilling the contents of his mug over Cousin Gnome. The squat man didn't seem to mind. "Ah, Aindréa! Welcome home! Did you have fun in the capital?"

"...What's going on here?"

"Funny thing, that!" Granda heartily slapped the gnome on his shoulder. "Turns out our languages have overlap with our tavern songs! Not a clue what his words mean, and he's not a clue of mine, but we've met in the middle!"

Granma blinked at him in silent confusion before gesturing broadly to the redesigned...everything. "I mean, what happened here? I only wanted you to clean the floors, not—"

"Do you like it, though? I know you wanted a remodel, but we hadn't the time. And here I learn that gnomes are savvy craftsmen! All this only took the better part of an afternoon! I say we welcome my cousin into the family proper, what say you?" Granda tilted his head back and bellowed a laugh, matched by Cousin Gnome.

Granma put her face in her hands and groaned.

Camaráin, though, leaned over to Ma and whispered, "Looks like praying for the best of luck worked."

Ma patted him on the head. "Maybe let Granma get used to the new help before we say that, huh?"

High spirits carried them all about their day. While Ma and Áine worked away in the kitchen to make tea and pastries, Camaráin sat on the couch with Brían in his lap, reading a piece of gnomish literature that had suddenly appeared in the house called *Crime and Gnomishment*. It was a dry read, so he only skimmed through the pages until he found himself staring at the "About the Author" page. It seemed it was written by a fellow named Gnomstoevsky...who bore a strange resemblance to Cousin Gnome. Probably a coincidence.

As finishing touches were put on the pastries and Granda and Cousin Gnome had a spirited discussion with Granma, a dense rapping at the door caught their attention. Ma rushed to the door, being the least occupied of those present, and opened the door to a startle.

"Eamon?" she said. "What are you doing here?"

Camaráin craned his head to see the former Inquisitor's tall form towering in the doorway, his head remaining out of view. A gauntleted hand held a scroll of paper.

"Good afternoon, Máirín. I've a letter for you."

"You're a fair ways from home, aren't you?"

"So are you."

"A shame, that. Having to put competent effort into your job must be hard."

"It is—hey, wait a minu—"

The door slammed shut before the minute could be thoroughly waited. Ma unrolled the paper, and her face lit up. She put a hand to her chest and was clearly fighting back tears.

"Ma?" Camaráin got off the couch, gently carrying Brían in his arms. He squinted to read the return address, seeing *One Draconic Highlands Terrace* scribbled in messy print. A stamp over the addressee line *Máirín of Baile* read in deep red ink: *MAIL FORWARDING. YES WE TAKE THIS VERY SERIOUSLY.* Camaráin tugged at Ma's trousers, eager of the letter's contents. "What is it? Who is it from?"

Ma put the letter down, a bright smile on her face. "It's from Ailís and Iósaf."

That drew everyone's attention. Granma and Granda rushed

over, forgetting whatever previous argument they had over Cousin Gnome, and huddled around the paper. Áine walked in with the fresh pastries, seeming to allow the family the space they needed.

Camaráin squeezed his way between Ma and Granma, and finally had the right angle to read the letter.

Dear Ma and Camaráin,

I miss you both a lot. Pilib and I have been learning a lot from the lorekeepers. At first I was scared, but all the dragons have been very nice to me, Ollepheist especially. He treats me like I'm his own family now that Pilib and I are Bonded. He says that in a year or two, Pilib might be big enough for me to ride on! That will be fun. I can't wait for that. We share lots of dreams now. Just wait until you can hear Pilib talk—he'll make you laugh all the time. I'll see you both someday soon.

Love,
Ailís

And, scribbled beneath that note was another.

Hey, you two. The kiddo's doing great. She's bright, inquisitive, asks all the right questions. She fits in perfectly here. You raised a real good one, Sis. Everything I've gleaned from the Great One and the lorekeepers suggests it'll be a few years yet, but once all her training's done, she's free to go anywhere she pleases. I'm sure the first stop will be right back to you both. Boy, if only I could see the faces on the Inquisitors when a full-grown dragon makes a stop in Baile. Hope they're wearing brown armor by that point, right?

Don't worry about us—or, I should probably say, don't worry about <u>her</u>. All's well here. See you soon.

Iósaf

As he finished the last of his uncle's note, confused by the bit about "brown armor," Camaráin felt himself crushed between the embrace of his ma and his grandparents. They were all overcome with emotion, happiness at hearing from Ailís and Iósaf both.

An additional set of hands found their way around Camaráin's shoulders. He expected them to be Áine's but was perplexed to see they were Cousin Gnome's. Áine's hands were instead wrapped around Ma's shoulders.

"You see?" she said, holding a plate with a freshly baked scone. "Not everything will be easy, but it will all be okay."

Ma seemed too overcome to respond properly, but she still managed an agreeing nod. Granma and Granda seemed to be in the same frame of mind, remarking to each other their elation at finally hearing from Uncle Iósaf again.

The scone was waiting unclaimed, so Camaráin happily took it and brought it back to the couch with Brían still nestled in the crest of his arm. As he sat back, he stared at the dragon, warmth radiating against his chest. Taking a bite of the scone—a heavenly bite, at that—Camaráin ran his hand down the length of Brían's ruby scales. Áine was right: though things were never easy, they would always turn out okay. No matter what happened.

He opened a new book called *Dragon Toward Its Natural Conclusion* and rested it against his thighs, Brían angling his head to follow along the pages. He was content. Surrounded by warmth, by family near and far, family of blood and of choice. It all felt right.

And as Brían trilled once more in his lap, it felt like home.

The End

A Message to the Reader

Welcome to the end of the book! I hope you enjoyed reading DRAGON ALONG.

If it's not too much trouble, I would greatly appreciate you leaving a review on Goodreads and/or Amazon. Reviews are important to authors (especially indie authors such as myself) as they enable us to expand our reach and let more people know that our books exist. Even a simple review saying, "I liked it!" is more than enough! And, most importantly, I'm just curious to know what you thought of this book! I hope to see you in the next one.

If you'd like to keep up with everything I'm doing, you can sign up for my monthly newsletter at joseph-john-lee.com.

Thank you,
Joe

Acknowledgements

Upscaled was a fun book to write. Dragon Along was a bit more challenging. As it turns out, no matter the genre, sequels are an odd sort to write, even for something so tongue-in-cheek and less-than-serious as this. It was no less fun to see come to life, but, as ever, it takes a village to get it to that point.

First, to my wonderful editor Sarah Chorn. Thank you as always for your hard work and enthusiasm in helping this book be all that it could be. Not only do you help make diamonds out of the dung I send your way, but your words are an incredible source of validation for when I'm questioning what the heck I'm even doing.

To the talented people at Miblart, thank you for your sterling work on the cover art for this book. It's due in part to your talents that Upscaled drew as many eyes as it did, and I am sure the same will be said of Dragon Along. The entire team is a treat to work with, and I'm always telling all my friends to work with you. (Hey friends, go work with Miblart!)

To Adam and Sammy, I'm always putting you two in here, and I've reached the end of what more I can say. But I can't have a book release without acknowledging the impact you've both had on me. Without your encouragement, I wouldn't be typing up an acknowledgements section for what is now the sixth(!) time. Thank you for being my first fans and my favorite fans.

To my favorite writing peeps – João, Sadir, Michael, Katie, Joe, Nic, Bethany, Morgan, James, Luke – you all make navigating the publishing waters far less lonely and far less frightening. I'm ever grateful to have you all as support through all the trials and tribulations of the writing world. Worst Generation but the Best Authors!

And finally, to my amazing wife, Annie. Your love, support, and tolerance toward me disappearing into the office to write for hours on end have long kept me encouraged to continue pursuing this dream. (And, as long as it means you get the TV to yourself to watch marathons of Real Housewives or The Traitors, I'd say it's a win-win for us both, right?) I'm eternally grateful to you, not only for supporting and championing my writing, but for supporting and championing me in all walks of our life, even if that life is just doing laundry and taxes together. You're the best, always.

Joseph John Lee is the fantasy author responsible for unleashing The Spellbinders and the Gunslingers trilogy and The Dragons of Nóra duology, and has been a semifinalist in Mark Lawrence's annual Self-Published Fantasy Blog-Off. A true product of New England, he prefers Dunkin' over Starbucks, sometimes speaks with a Boston accent, and does not say the word "wicked" in casual conversation as much as one may think. He currently lives in Boston with his wife, Annie, and their robot vacuum named Crumb.